MARIE-HÉLÈNE LEBEAULT

THE TIME WALKER

THE EVERS SERIES BOOK THREE

BEACHES AND TRAILS
PUBLISHING

This book is dedicated to my parents, Jocelyne and Pierre, and to my American relatives, the Crimbolis, for buying and reading a series of Young Adult Fantasy novels. You're the best!

ACKNOWLEDGEMENT

To my good friend Denise Drolet, I declare my undying gratitude. Thank you for reading my drafts, providing insightful comments, being the best cheerleader, buying the books, and raving about them to everyone! And finally, a shout out to Hilde Pols, my NaNoWriMo buddy, for her ongoing support.

I

SIBLINGS

"**D**id that just happen?" asked Lola, shell-shocked, the injured finger in her mouth. Devlin was still holding the piece of parchment, staring blankly at it.

"Yes, we are siblings . . ." he agreed blankly.

The nurse gathered her effects, did a quick mini-curtsy to the Headmaster, and took her leave.

"Well, that's settled. Isn't it good news?" asked the Headmaster.

Lola and Devlin wore identical shocked expressions.

Smiling from one to the other, the Headmaster blanched visibly as a thought occurred to him. "You're not dating each other, are you?" he asked aghast, rushing towards them.

They both cried, "No!" and then started laughing. Suddenly, the spell was broken.

"That's a relief. It would have been an unfortunate turn of events," said the Headmaster, running a hand through his silky silver hair. He put a hand on Lola's shoulder and asked, "Are you alright?"

She shot a glance at Devlin, then looked up into the Headmaster's serene face. "Yes. I'm just surprised. Though I really shouldn't be after everything that's happened in the last few months," admitted Lola, throwing up her hands. She glanced over at Devlin, smiled, and added, "But I'm very happy to have a brother!"

Devlin locked eyes with her and a huge grin spread over his face. "And I have a sister. And a family! I won't have to be on my own," said Devlin, getting up quickly.

Lola rose and faced him. "I can't wait for you to meet Phyllis!" Lola said, excited now. Devlin grabbed Lola and wrapped her in a bear hug. Lola responded by wrapping her own arms around his waist. They hugged tightly for a minute or so then separated, still holding hands.

"Headmaster, do you think you could write to my aunt and break the news to her before she comes tomorrow?" asked Lola. "It might be easier. My aunt also has a tendency to faint . . ." she trailed.

"Yes, of course, of course," he murmured, nodding absently as he headed back towards his desk. His lithe frame eased into the chair, then he grabbed a quill and parchment and started writing immediately. Then, realizing Lola and Devlin were still just standing there, he looked up and said, "I think that's enough excitement for one day. I shall write to your aunt presently. Am I correct in presuming you would like to picnic together?"

Lola and Devlin both nodded. "I had already invited Devlin to join us since he had no one to visit him," explained Lola. "Now, it'll be an even bigger surprise!" she added, beaming. She looked down at their clasped hands. Devlin looked down as well and, as though realizing this was a bit much, they let go.

"Indeed," replied the Headmaster ruefully. "Why don't you both go enjoy the rest of the afternoon with your friends. If I have any more news or information to impart, I'll let you know at dinnertime." He waved them away and started writing to Phyllis.

"Yes, Headmaster," said Devlin, heading for the door.

"Thank you so much, sir," said Lola, following Devlin out the door and down the stairs.

They said nothing as they reached the landing and headed towards the Main Hall door. All the students were meant to be outside. Devlin checked his watch and frowned.

"What is it?" asked Lola, stopping once they were outside.

"It is already four. We have probably missed the group activities. What do you want to do?" inquired Devlin.

Lola shielded her eyes from the sun and her gaze swept the lawns. She could see groups of students here and there, talking, throwing a football, or practicing spells. In the distance, she could see the girls sunning in the lounge chairs.

When she looked back at Devlin, she saw he was looking at the guys. They were kicking a soccer ball in a circle. She could tell that Devlin was itching to join them.

"Do you want to go play soccer, I mean football, with the guys?" asked Lola.

"I do. But I really don't want to have to answer questions about where I was this whole time," he said.

"I know! I'm dying for a nap, but there's no way I could just plop down on a chair unnoticed," replied Lola.

They both looked towards the meditation platform, nodded, and started walking.

Two hours ago, they had been having fun at the BBQ with their friends. It was Saturday at the Academy, one week into their very first two-week Summer Program.

The Academy was a University for Traveling Students: students who, with a magic key, could open doors to anywhere in the world. Some Travelers, like Lola, were also Time Walkers: Travelers who could open a door to anywhere, *and any time*. A rare few, like Devlin, were World Jumpers: Travelers who could Travel to and from other worlds and dimensions.

In the summer, the Academy opened its doors to students from thirteen to eighteen years old so they could learn how to use their keys safely and appropriately. The curriculum included History, Latin, Magic, Traveling, Martial Arts, Meditation, and Magical Communities. These classes were also prerequisites to attend the University. Any Traveler who had attended the Summer Program and completed their

Secondary education could attend the University. However, attendance was mandatory for potential Custodians—Travelers who were the last of their family line. Custodian duties were still nebulous.

Both Lola, sixteen, and Devlin, eighteen, had been summoned to the Academy a handful of days before Orientation, following the deaths of their remaining parents. Lola's mother had died of cancer while they were living in Baltimore. She was sent to live in a mansion in the deep south with her aunt Phyllis Evers. Phyllis was her father's sister, whom Lola had last seen when she was two years old and obviously didn't remember her. Devlin's mother had died in a car crash and he had no living relatives.

Their parents had not attended the Academy, and neither of them knew anything at all about Keys or Traveling before their parents' deaths. But they were all caught up now after spending a week cramming five summers' worth of classes so they could be ready for the fall semester.

Today was their first day off. They were meant to be relaxing and having fun. Instead, they had just spent the last two hours with the Headmaster who, finding the circumstances of their arrival, their mothers' deaths, and their rare abilities a bit too coincidental, had started investigating. The result of this investigation was finding out that they had both been fathered by Simon Bartholomew Evers. Lola had grown up without her father because, like her mother, he had died of cancer when she was two. However, after she had arrived at the Mansion, Simon had time-traveled so he could spend some time with his daughter but had disappeared on her sixteenth birthday. For his part, Devlin had been told his father had died before he was born and his mother had never discussed him.

*

As they neared the meditation platform, they saw it was already in use. Since they had a lot to talk about, Devlin nodded toward the Greenhouse and they set off again in companionable silence. They headed for Lola's favorite bench and sat down. The last time they had been here was when they had gone flying with Professor Elderberry. On impulse, Lola turned to see if she could spot the fairy in the Greenhouse or buzzing about the gardens but couldn't see her.

"Tell me about Simon and Phyllis," murmured Devlin.

Lola turned to face him on the bench and smiled.

"Phyllis is like a fairy godmother! But she's not a fairy, obviously," replied Lola and they both laughed and relaxed.

Lola told him about her bus ride to Williamsburg, the car ride with Jackson, and the welcome she got when she had arrived at the Mansion. She described the house and the Estate. There were extensive details about the food, which Devlin lapped up like a starving man. She told him about their father, his paintings, and his bond with Phyllis. She talked about her own relationship with Phyllis and how she was sorry he had missed not only meeting their dad, but also the huge birthday party.

"We'll have to throw another one, to introduce you to society too!" she exclaimed.

"I'm sure that is not necessary. Just having a home and a family is more than enough for me," he replied wistfully.

"Well, at least you already know how to dance. You'll be on everyone's guest list in no time," quipped Lola and they laughed again.

Growing serious again, Lola explained how she was told that there are usually two children, a boy, and a girl, in every generation of the Evers.

"Now it makes sense!" she said. "I guess that makes you the Custodian as well as an heir," she added.

"I don't care about money. I can get a job and pay my own way," he replied stiffly.

"Now I know we're related. That's exactly what I said!" Lola cried. "Until I found out there was so much to do and, honestly, so much money that managing it is someone's job," she continued.

"Would that be Jackson?" asked Devlin.

"Yes. He and Phyllis are doing it together until he gets his degree, but he's really good at it," said Lola.

"And what else is he good at?" asked Devlin, wiggling his brows.

Lola's face turned beet-red and she mock-slapped him. "Stop it!"

They grew serious after a while. Devlin was staring off into space while Lola was studying his profile, trying to catch a glimpse of Simon. But he just looked like Devlin to her.

"Do you think she will like me?" he asked, barely above a whisper.

"Phyllis?" she asked, and he nodded.

"Of course she will! She'll be overjoyed at another family member. She's been so lonely since Simon died. I bet she's already prepping one of the bedrooms for you. When I got there, she had a whole wardrobe ready for me. But I'm thinking that's a girl thing. If you come and live with us, she won't feel so guilty about spending time with Boris, her boyfriend. Or about leaving Jackson and me unchaperoned . . ." said Lola.

"Indeed, you should NOT be spending too much time alone with any boy. But certainly not one who basically lives with you. At least here at school, there is no privacy so couples can't get into too much trouble. On that note, what are you going to do about Jackson and Tom?" he asked.

Lola exhaled deeply and shrugged.

"I have no idea," she confessed.

2

RELATED

When the chime rang, indicating the students could go back to the dorms to wash and change for dinner, Lola and Devlin got up and headed back to the Main Hall. Since they were closer, they arrived among the first students and didn't see any of their friends. They hadn't decided on how or when they would tell them they were newfound siblings. Devlin didn't have a roommate, so he knew he was in the clear until dinner. Sara, however, would certainly grill Lola. Both Lola and Devlin had been called to see the Headmaster on more than one occasion. Surely that would be a good enough explanation for now.

In the end, it was a moot point. Lola had time to shower and change before Sara arrived. She was heading out the door as her roommate arrived and said they'd catch up at dinner. Since she was a little early, Lola headed for the Common Room where she promptly collided with Tom. They grabbed at each other awkwardly, then laughed and decided on a proper hug. Pulling back, Tom asked, "Where were you all afternoon?"

Lola bit her lip and pushed imaginary pebbles with her shoe. "Um . . . I was with . . . the Headmaster," she replied tentatively. Tom's eyes bore into hers. He raised an eyebrow, waiting for more. She glanced back behind her, checking if they were alone. Then bent around him to check the Common Room. Catching her gaze, he suggested, "I like a good mystery! Let's go to the Library," already tugging her by the hand. They headed straight for the wing-back chairs near the back of the Library. Once he had her in the seat, he gave her an intense gaze and said, "Talk." When she said nothing at first, he added, "I noticed Devlin was missing as well and I'd like an explanation before jumping to conclusions," through gritted teeth.

That spurred her on. "I was, but it's really not what you're thinking!" she said quickly.

"You spend quite a lot of time alone together. Studying, talking quietly, meeting early in the morning, and coming back to the dorms late at night," he commented.

"Wow, stalk much?" she replied defensively.

"Stalk, no. Observe, yes. You have to admit it looks like you might fancy one another, which is fine, but I don't want to get mixed up in a triangle," he said somberly.

Lola let out a nervous giggle and immediately put a hand to her mouth in horror.

"I'm sorry. I'm nervous. I could see how you would think that. But seriously, that's not it at all," she said, regaining her composure.

"Well, spit it out already, can't you see I'm dying here?" he said, gesturing wildly.

"He's my brother," she stated.

"What?" replied Tom incredulously.

"We've only JUST found out. That's why we've been spending so much time with the Headmaster. As to spending so much time together, we DID have a lot of studying to do and we're new here, and we're in a two-person class all day, every day. Even under normal circumstances, that would be enough for two people to bond. But now that I know he's my brother, well, half-brother actually, it makes sense that we had an instant rapport," she explained.

"Unbelievable! And you've only just found out. Have you told anyone?" he asked.

"You're the first," she said with a wan expression.

"I'm honored. And now I feel like an ass, assaulting you with my pointed questions when you're probably still reeling from the shock. Come here, brave girl," he said, getting up and opening his arms. As though in a trance, Lola got up and fitted her face in the crook of his neck and breathed. His arms came around her for a tight, but brief squeeze. This was no time for seduction. This was a time for support. He kissed the top of her hair and released her. "Better?" he asked. "Much," was her reply. Lola was about to sit down again when the lights blinked. "Dinner!" they both said and rushed out of the Library and into the Dining Room with seconds to spare. The Headmaster was about to address the assembly.

"Good evening, children. I hope you enjoyed this afternoon's activities," he started, and a cheer erupted from the room. He raised a hand and everyone quieted once more.

"This evening, an outdoor theater will be set up on the West Lawn. Snacks will be provided and you may wear your own clothing for the event," he said and paused while the cheers renewed.

"The movie, *The Extraordinary Adventures of Adèle Blanc-Sec*, will commence promptly at eight p.m. Curfew has not been extended, so you are expected back in your rooms immediately after the movie ends. Therefore, dinner will end at seven-thirty this evening.

"Finally, a reminder. Tomorrow, the breakfast buffet will be available from six-thirty to nine-thirty for those of you who may want to sleep in. Lunch will be picnic hampers to share with your visitors. Visiting hours are from one to four p.m. You and your family may retrieve your hampers from the Gazebo on the West Lawn. Dinner will be served at the usual hour. Enjoy!" concluded the Headmaster heading back to his seat as the assembly applauded.

While the platters were brought in, the students discussed whether anyone had seen the movie or not. Only Clara had seen it and declared it was a great pick, though she worried about some of the younger students.

"Why? Is it scary? Gross?" asked Lola, a little worried herself.

"Let's just say there are a few scenes that are not for the faint at heart. But don't worry, it's still considered a family movie," explained Clara.

Though Clara's endorsement did nothing to calm Lola's nerves, it certainly sparked interest in the rest of the group.

"Who's got a date? I know I do!" said Lenora with a wink. Automatically, Colin and James raised their hands and everybody cracked up. Clara said she was going with Gunther, a boy at the end of their table. She blew him a kiss when he turned on hearing his name.

"Um, Tom asked me to sit with him," said Lola, shyly.

This got a round of catcalls and wolf whistles from around the table. To deflect the attention away from her red cheeks, Lola nudged Devlin and gave a nod towards Sara. He looked panicked, so she scooted forward to ask Colin for seconds. That way Devlin could lean over behind her and ask Sara if she would sit with him.

"Sara?" Devlin asked.

"What?" she replied.

"Would you sit with me for the movie?" he asked with a shy smile.

"I would love to!" she replied, beaming.

Devlin patted Lola's back to indicate she could lean back again and whispered, "Thanks, she said yes!" Lola smiled at Devlin and Sara in turn and dug into her second plate of spaghetti and meatballs, so very pleased with herself.

"I am going to the movie with Sara," exclaimed Devlin, puffing out his chest proudly.

"Well done," said James with a wink. Colin was eyeing the lot of them suspiciously.

"If Lola is going with Tom and Sara is going with Devlin, would you mind explaining to us where the two of you were all afternoon?" asked Colin, pointing with his fork.

Everyone stopped talking as it became apparent that they must have been together.

Lola and Devlin looked at each other and shrugged.

"It is a long story, but Lola is my sister," blurted Devlin to an array of shocked and disbelieving faces. Lola sighed and proceeded to tell them most of what had happened since her mom died. Devlin added his bits of information.

"*C'est incroyable!*" gasped Clara, returning to her native French. "You do not look alike at all," she added, frowning.

The gang had a ton of questions and Lola and Devlin filled in as many blanks as they could as they had tiramisu for dessert. Soon, the lights were blinking and it was time to change and head for the outdoor theater.

In their room, Sara and Lola were changing quickly and there wasn't much time to talk as they were putting extra effort into their appearance. Lola actually brushed out her hair and put on a bit of gloss. Sara was impressed. She was wearing full makeup, dangling earrings, and her chestnut hair was up into a sexy bun with loose tendrils framing her face. She looked like a supermodel. Lola gave a whistle and Sara smiled shyly. "Is it too much?" she asked.

"You're asking the wrong girl!" said Lola. "But I'm pretty sure Devlin would like you even if you were wearing a clown suit!" she added. "How about me?"

"If you were going for wholesome, you nailed it!" quipped Sara, then putting her arms around her friend as they faced the mirror, she added, "Absolutely perfect!"

Devlin and Tom were waiting on the landing at the end of the stairs. Now that it was clear they were not competing for the same girl, they seemed relaxed and companionable. When the girls reached them, they each offered an arm and led them outside.

As they neared the West Lawn, they saw the huge screen, surrounded by twinkle lights.

To the right, there was an old-fashioned popcorn cart, and a server was handing out cartons of buttery popcorn. To the left were a candy stand and a self-serve soda fountain. The seating was divided into three sections. At the front, there were blankets set up with cushions. A second row had lounge chairs and the third row had benches.

The boys led them to blankets they had already reserved and asked if that was alright. Lola would have preferred the lounge chairs, as they were more comfortable. But the blankets were more romantic. She smiled and nodded. Sara nodded too. It seemed all the older kids had the same idea because soon they saw Colin and James grab one. Then Clara and Gunther plopped down a few blankets over, and finally Lenora and her date. Lola asked Tom who the guy was, and he said, "That's Keith. He's a friend." He frowned.

"What's wrong?" Lola asked.

"She doesn't usually date younger guys, and Keith hasn't dated much. I hope she won't chew him up and spit him out," he replied.

"Maybe they're just friends?" suggested Lola.

Tom shrugged and turned back to Lola. A slow smile crept up his face. "You look lovely, as always," he said, giving her a brief kiss on the cheek.

Lola beamed and replied, "Thank you. You're quite dashing yourself!"

He took her hand, and they settled on the blanket to watch the movie.

3

SUNDAY

Once her morning routine was done, Lola went down to breakfast and was pleasantly surprised to see Tom at their table, waiting for her with Devlin. Both boys got up when she arrived. She blushed and sat between them. Tom poured her a cup of coffee and Devlin poured her a glass of apple juice.

"What's going on? Why are you both being so nice to me?" she asked warily, looking from one to the other.

Devlin cleared his throat. "Is it not a brother's job to take care of his little sister?" he asked innocently. Lola narrowed her eyes at him, pursed her lips, and said, "Sure, thanks." Turning to Tom, she crossed her arms and asked, "What's your excuse?"

Tom looked earnestly into Lola's face and smiled. He tucked a strand of hair behind her ear and replied, "You deserve to have people do nice things for you."

Lola opened her mouth to speak and closed it. Twice. Then, realizing she would not get a straight answer out of either of them, she smiled, leaned back in her chair and announced, "I'd like a Belgian waffle topped with cinnamon sugar, with a dollop of whipped cream in the middle, and sprinkled with summer berries."

It took a second or two for them to react, but then Tom shot up and left to fetch her food from the buffet. Devin was snapping his fingers; he hadn't been fast enough. Lola's smile widened. "I'd also like three or four slices of bacon, a pat of butter, some raspberry jam, a croissant, and a slice of Havarti cheese," she added, pointedly looking at Devlin. His chair screeched as he left.

Lola was enjoying her coffee, humming to herself, when Colin and James sat down in front of her.

"Why do you look like the cat that ate the canary?" asked James with a smile.

"Because, for a reason they have yet to reveal to me, Tom and Devlin are acting like my own personal slaves," she responded with a hair toss, which she obviously did not pull off because Colin said, "You need to toss it faster and have to make snooty face to get the full effect, like this." Colin mimed it for her and she burst out laughing, and coffee streamed out of her nose. Horrified, she grabbed her napkin and covered her face as she mopped up the coffee off it then from the table. Colin and James were in stitches, and James almost spat his orange juice out. Just then Devlin and Tom arrived back with her food.

"I brought you a little maple syrup for the waffle," said Tom, putting the plate in front of her and raising an eyebrow at the coffee stain on the table cloth. She gave him a *don't ask* scowl, and he sat down with his own plate of food.

Meanwhile, Devlin deposited his offering next to her other plate and sat down to eat his own breakfast. Colin and James went to fill their plates and when they came back, Colin casually asked what time they were meeting to play W&W.

Both Devlin and Tom looked up, identical guilty looks on their faces.

"Ah, that's why you were being so nice to me. You're both leaving me to play with the guys," she said, laughing. "I really don't mind! I might go back to sleep and I've been wanting some girl time with Sara," she said. Then, turning to Devlin, she added, "I'll meet you a little before one in the Main Hall, okay?" Devlin nodded and smiled gratefully.

Lola turned to Tom. "I love spending time with you, but we don't need to spend all our time together. I'm not some needy, high-maintenance girl. We can find some time after the picnic to go for a walk or something," she suggested.

"Sounds great, Lola. Thank you," replied Tom.

Lola resumed eating and when she was done, she motioned at her dishes and said, "You guys will take care of these for me, right?" Not waiting for a response, she got up, kissed Tom on the cheek, and left.

Back in the room, Lola had a nice nap and woke up at the same time as Sara. After getting a cup of coffee from the girl's Sitting Room and grabbing a granola bar from her contraband stash, Sara was ready for a gabfest. There was so much to talk about!

"How was your date with Devlin?" asked Lola, sitting cross-legged on Sara's bed.

Sara finished chewing and replied, "It's not really what I would call a date. We sat together on a blanket and watched a PG film."

"What would you do on a date back home?" asked Lola.

"Well, if we did go see a film, we wouldn't be chaperoned by the entire school, for one thing," she replied and they both laughed. "But seriously, we'd probably go for a cuppa or a bite to eat, someplace where we could talk and get to know one another," she said.

"Tom and I went for a walk yesterday morning. Seems like forever ago considering so many things have happened since," said Lola, remembering how their hands had intertwined. "How do I know if we're in a relationship?" she asked suddenly.

Sara made an *O* with her mouth and sat up straighter. This was a serious discussion.

"You really are a novice, aren't you?" she asked.

"Yes! All I know is what I've seen on tv or in movies, but I doubt any of that is accurate or fits with my situation!" wailed Lola, putting her face into her hands.

"Don't fret, love. I'm here to help," responded Sara, clapping her hands and rubbing them together. "First, you'll know he is your boyfriend when you both agree that you are dating exclusively. Have you had that talk with Tom? How about Jackson?" she asked Lola.

Lola looked up and shook her head. "Jackson insisted that I should be free to date, or rather accept invitations to dances and parties, so I would have more choices. That's also what my aunt Phyllis suggested when I said I liked Jackson just fine. Of course, that was when I thought I had to marry to ensure the continuation of the Evers line. Now, not only does that seem like an outdated practice meant to keep old money in the right circles, but I'm no longer the heir! I'm the spare!" said Lola enthusiastically.

"You mean because Devlin is older?" asked Sara.

"Exactly!" said Lola.

"Doesn't that mean you lose the house and the money? And wouldn't he need to be legitimate to inherit anything? I'm not a barrister but I'm pretty sure people need to be named in a will to inherit and children can't be illegitimate," replied Sara.

"The heir is meant to take over as Custodian and is required to live in the house. They are also supposed to get married and have two children, a boy, and a girl. As an Evers, I can live in the house forever if I want. And I'd get the same inheritance regardless. The difference is that I'm free to live where I want, marry who I want or not at all, and am not at all responsible for the Estate!" said Lola, her tone increasing in level more and more. "I can't believe how happy I am about this. I hadn't realized how daunting the task was because I thought I'd be sharing it with Jackson," she said, leaning back on the wall and stretching out her legs in front of her. "As to the illegitimacy thing, I doubt my aunt will give a rip and I certainly don't, so unless there's a law against it, I say Devlin is the heir!" said Lola joyfully.

Sara had been smiling with her friend, happy that the stress seemed to be draining from her shoulders. But now a frown was forming on her brow.

"Lola, does that mean that whoever marries Devlin is expected to produce two children and live in Virginia?" asked Sara. When Lola nodded emphatically, Sara gulped. "I mean, we like each other and we went on one non-date. It's not like we're getting married or anything. I'd just like to know what I'm getting into . . ."

"Don't worry, I get it! I was such a fool for Jackson, that I just went along with everybody's plans that we should marry in a few years, pop out a couple of kids and live Happily Ever After! Seriously! Who gets married to the first boy they kiss?" asked Lola.

"I'm sure it happens, now and again. But I agree with you. It's much too soon for either of us to be discussing marriage, babies, and Estates! What an utter bore! I much prefer talking about how many boys we can kiss before having to settle on just one so they don't get jealous!" giggled Sara. Lola was laughing too. "Wait, how many boys CAN you kiss at the same time?" asked Lola. Sara wiggled her eyebrows and said, "If you're doing it right, only ONE at a time." Lola laughed and pretended to kick Sara. "Stop that! You know what I mean. And are we obligated to discuss said kissing with other boys we may have kissed or are considering kissing?" she asked earnestly.

"Never kiss and tell, that's my motto," replied Sara. "Unless you get caught, then honesty is the best policy," she conceded.

"So what do I do about Jackson?" said Lola, anxiously. "I mean, he has no idea how much things have changed in the past week. He doesn't know about Devlin. He knows very little about the whole key and Traveling business, but he knows enough to understand he'll be out of a job and home if I get married to someone else. Technically, that would also be the outcome if Devlin becomes the heir. So he's bound to freak out about the whole thing. I really don't think I should mention Tom . . ."

"You are overthinking this. Just ask yourself this: If you take away all the back story, do you like Jackson, for Jackson. How do you feel when you're around him? Which part of you shows up? What about Tom? And remember, it's not an either/ or situation. When fall comes around, there will be even more boys here to choose from!" said Sara with a wink.

"I guess I'll have to think about it," replied Lola, unsure. Sara mock-slapped her arm.

"No, silly. Don't think. How do you feel? Close your eyes and give me one feeling word for Jackson," insisted Sara raising her voice slightly.

Lola complied. Once her eyes were closed, she pictured Jackson in her mind and said, "Safe."

"Okay, now keep those eyes closed and give me a feeling word for Tom," said Sara, more calmly.

Lola took a deep breath and exhaled. "Relaxed," came her reply.

"Good. Now, let's be practical in our analysis. How's the kissing?" asked Sara, cheekily.

Lola blushed and was saved from having to go into details by the sound of the chime. It was noon and time to change and get ready for the picnic.

4

PICNIC

In the end, Phyllis took it quite well. She welcomed Devlin with open arms and treated him to her usual southern charm. She remarked that though Devlin didn't resemble Simon all that much, he did bear a striking resemblance to her father. She promised to send pictures and asked about his favorite colors and pastimes so she could prepare a room for him when he came home with Lola.

They had a lovely picnic near the woods. The basket had included a large blanket to sit on, some finger sandwiches, crudités, cheese cubes, grapes, cherries, and a thermos of iced tea. It was delicious and they had fun talking about the first week of 'camp.' Phyllis said she had spent a few days with Boris at his home in Moscow.

At about two-thirty, Tom found them and Lola introduced him to Phyllis. He sat and chatted with them for a while, then suggested he and Lola go for a short stroll. Everyone agreed and they left. Left on their own, Phyllis and Devlin got to know one another better.

Phyllis asked about his mother, his childhood, and inquired if he had any artistic talents. Devlin said he liked to dance and was good at sketching portraits, though he'd never had a chance to paint. Phyllis told him he could use Simon's studio and see if he had a knack for it.

"Are you sure it is alright for me to move in with you? You don't even know me," Devlin said, anxiously.

"The Headmaster explained about the blood tests. And, as I said, you look a lot like my father. I admit I was surprised when he wrote to me. But considering Simon's eccentricities, I shouldn't be all that surprised. Besides, there have always been two children, a boy, and a girl, born in every generation of Evers. It makes perfect sense to me!" replied Phyllis. "Though I should mention that I have discussed the matter with our attorneys and they may request a regular paternity test at some point. But I can't imagine it would say any different from the one you've had already. It'll just make things official," she added, nonplussed.

"You are as generous and as gracious as Lola has described. And you are even more beautiful than she said!" he said in a rush.

"Well, aren't you the charmer? You'll fit right in! Come here and give your old aunt a squeeze!" she said, opening her arms to him. He was so tall, it was easier for him to wrap his arms around her. They laughed and resumed their chat.

"I'm assuming you and Lola will be free to go next Sunday at some point. I don't think they'll have visiting hours if the program is done. How about you send your things with Lola's? When you get here, we'll give you the grand tour, and set you up in your room. On Monday, or whenever is convenient, we can all go with you to your home in Sweden and help you pack more of your things. We can arrange for the sale of your home, or if you prefer to keep it, we can have it rented out. Jackson will help. You know about Jackson, don't you?" she asked.

"Yes, Lola has spoken about him," he replied. "And thank you. That sounds like a good plan."

"Don't mention it. You're family!" she said warmly. "Now, tell me about the boy Tom!" She winked conspiratorially.

Devlin gave her the scoop, as he knew it, about Tom and Lola. He promised her he was keeping an eye on Tom to ensure he behaved appropriately. Phyllis stifled a laugh at his earnest expression and thanked him for it.

As if on cue, Tom and Lola returned and, before leaving, Tom told

Phyllis about his upcoming birthday party and how both Lola and Devlin were invited. He slipped her a piece of paper. "This is my address with my mother's name and number if you want to talk to her," he said with a smile. He told them to enjoy the rest of their picnic and went back to join his own family.

"He's a charming boy. Where did you two go off to?" asked Phyllis.

"He took me to meet his mom and sister, Tabitha. They were very welcoming," replied Lola.

"I'll definitely feel better about this house party if Devlin is with you," said Phyllis. "Well now, perhaps we should pack up the basket and drop it off somewhere. It's almost time to go, and I promised the Headmaster I'd have a word with him before I left."

They packed up and headed for the Main Hall. On the way, they dropped off the basket at a table set up for just that purpose and went into the Hall. Phyllis hugged each of them in turn and said she was already looking forward to having them home next week. When she was about to walk towards the Headmaster's office, he arrived in the Hall and took her arm to lead her away. She waved at the children and disappeared with the Headmaster.

More families were headed their way, so Lola and Devlin decided to change location. They headed towards the Common Room and sat down in the leather armchairs by the fireplace. They talked about the picnic, Phyllis's plans for his arrival, and about what they each had planned for the rest of the summer.

Their friends, and other students, started trickling in and they hung out until it was time for dinner. No one needed to shower or change. It was nice to kick back and relax. Lola and Devlin were looking forward to an evening off.

5

FRIDAY

The second week flew by. Lola and Devlin continued their semi-private classes during the day and their evenings of cramming in the Library. Every morning they brought one of their friends for a flight experience with Professor Elderberry. Everyone loved it except Clara, who was terribly sick afterward and never wanted to do it again. Professor Elderberry was very pleased to have a steady stream of morning helpers to look for in the fall.

By Friday, they were happy to be done with it and to have caught up with their classmates. In the fall, Tom and Lola would be finishing high school while the rest of them would begin their college-level classes. They would, however, all begin their Traveling-related classes together.

At lunch on Friday, the Headmaster announced the Social theme was Winter Wonderland. While he said it was a favorite with the younger kids, everyone roared with applause at the news. Lola and Devlin wore curious expressions but clapped with the others.

"As a reminder, on Saturday and Sunday, the breakfast buffet will be available from six-thirty to nine-thirty for those of you who may want to sleep in. Lunch on Saturday will be an outdoor BBQ, available on the West Lawn from twelve-thirty to two-thirty. In the afternoon, long chairs and parasols will be set up on the South Lawn for those wishing to bask in the sun. Collective sports will be organized on the East Lawn, and those wanting silence and solitude may use the Meditation platform on the North Lawn. Dinner tomorrow will be served at the usual hour, followed by movie night . . ."

This brought on another round of applause.

"Finally, departure on Sunday will begin at eleven for the thirteen-year-olds, eleven-thirty for the fourteen-year-olds, noon for the fifteen-year-olds, and twelve-thirty for the older students. There will be no lunch service.

"Before you leave, make sure you drop all items of your uniform in the chute to be laundered and stored. Take all of your personal effects with you so we can clean the rooms thoroughly. For those returning in the fall, please see Professor Kravchuk. He will have your information packets. Registration must be returned before August 15."

The Headmaster went to his seat and lunch was served.

As they ate, Lola asked if everyone had the same major or if there were choices.

"My older brother said there are five to choose from: Global Studies, International Affairs, International Management, Linguistics, and Liberal Arts," said Clara.

"Does everybody know what major they'll be choosing?" asked Devlin.

Sara and Clara said they were going for Liberal Arts. Colin was choosing International Management. James said he was thinking of Linguistics because he had an affinity for languages. Lenora wanted to do International Affairs.

"You know that's not having affairs with international students," quipped Colin.

"Haha. I know perfectly well what the program entails and I think you'll find I'm a natural at it," replied Lenora, only slightly miffed.

"How about you, Devlin?" asked Lola.

"Either Global Studies or Liberal Arts, I think. I will need to look over the course list," he replied. "And you, Lola?" he asked.

"Probably Liberal Arts. I want to be a writer. But I admit Linguistics seems appealing as well," she answered. "When does school start?"

"We're due back on the first Sunday in September. That gives us a whole month off!" exclaimed Sara.

That got them talking about their summer plans. Other than Tom's party, Colin and James were hoping to have people over at some point and would be in touch.

"Will you text or send one of those origami letters?" asked Lola, curious.

Everyone laughed.

"Text, definitely text. We only used the origami at school, or to and from the Academy. I mean, it works everywhere. Some people use it to send letters instead of through the post. But I'm quite sure we all have cell phones," said Colin with a smirk.

"My brothers and sisters use them a lot. So do my parents and their friends," replied Clara.

"Just give your details to Sara and she'll share them with the rest of us," said James to Lola and Devlin.

That afternoon, Master Smoke offered to test the younger students who were interested in being graded. He explained that children under sixteen could also receive Gray, Yellow, Orange, and Green belts which were intermediate belts between White and Blue. The reason they were officially tested at the end of camp, was so they could continue their instruction at another studio during the rest of the year. As Lola was the only sixteen-year-old student in the group, Master Smoke asked her to pair with her usual partner so that the others could continue with their grading. She asked if she could be included in the testing to measure her progress.

In the end, had Lola been eligible, she would have received an Orange Belt, and she was quite pleased. There was no way she would pursue Brazilian Jiu-Jitsu on her own, but she was happy to have improved and mastered enough of the basics to use them if the need arose.

For their last M&M class, Professor Brambles told them a short story after their group meditation.

"*One day, a strong young man came to a lumberjack camp looking for a job. Seeing his appearance, the manager hired him without hesitation. He did an excellent job on the first day, and everyone was happy with his performance.*

"*Strangely, on the second day, his production lessened by half, even though he had worked just as hard. On the third day, his results were even worse. He only felled a few trees.*

"*When they asked him about his poor performance, the young man answered that he didn't know what was happening. He had worked just as hard every day. Then his boss asked him a question: When was the last time you sharpened your axe? The boy replied that he hadn't found the time. He was too busy felling trees.*"

As usual, she asked the students to share their insight on the story and ended the class with the following advice:

"Don't forget to Sharpen Your Axe, meaning to increase your personal productivity by having a balanced strategy to renew yourself in the four aspects of life: Physical, Social, Mental, and Spiritual. Enjoy your vacation and use the next four weeks well!"

She bade them farewell and told them to enjoy the remaining days on campus.

6

WONDERLAND

O n the Friday night, dinner was a hot lamb stew, fresh bread, a green salad, and an olive and cheese platter. For dessert, they had a sticky fig and pecan pudding with toffee sauce.

After dinner, everyone went to change and met on the front lawn. There, Master Smoke had them line up as they usually did for Martial Arts class. But instead of three mini-temples, there was one large mini-castle behind him with three doorways.

Lola and Tom were standing together. She was really excited. Tom didn't say a word because he didn't want to give away the surprise. When they crossed the threshold of the castle, their clothes changed into winter apparel with mittens, hats, scarves, and boots!

Astonished, Lola looked up at Tom and grinned. He smiled and nodded ahead of them. They weren't really in a castle, but more of a courtyard. In the middle of the courtyard, there was a huge frozen pond and students were rushing to get some skates and try it out. All around the pond were little food carts offering hot chocolate, roasted chestnuts, gingerbread men, and frosted sugar cookies. There was also a huge snow globe to take pictures next to.

Devlin walked out with Sara and he looked like a kid in a candy store. They were heading towards Lola and Tom when they heard loud whooping behind them. Colin and James were sitting in a small sleigh being pulled by what looked like a reindeer.

"No way," said Lola, jaw hanging slack.

"Lola, look!" said Devlin pointing further behind the ice rink. There was a steep hill and students were sliding down the hill on yellow tubes. Lola grabbed Tom's hand and pulled him towards the hill, laughing all the way. Devlin and Sara were close behind, whooping like children.

Luckily there was only a short line and their History teacher was there holding out tubes to arriving students.

"Hello, Dr. McClary!" said Lola politely when it was their turn.

"Hello, Lola, are you enjoying yourself?" he asked, handing her a tube.

"I don't think I've ever had so much fun in my life. This is amazing! I love Magic!" she exclaimed. The teacher laughed and waved her off. They headed up the four flights of stairs of the wooden structure that led to the hill. One after the other, depending on how brave they were, they would either sit in the tube hole and be pushed down or leave at a run and hop on the tube as they went. The latter was much faster. They went at least five times in a row before the stairs got to them, and they decided to take a break and do something else. Tom suggested a sleigh ride. Lola expressed her opinion by clapping her hands and jumping up and down.

"I was going to suggest a cup of hot chocolate and a cookie for the ride, but I'm not sure you should be ingesting any sugar. You are on too much of a high as it is!" said Tom, laughing.

"Blasphemy!" replied Lola, joyfully pulling him towards the ginger-bread men stand.

Each of the gingerbread cookies, because there were men and women, was decorated differently and it was difficult to choose as they were very beautifully decorated. Lola picked a girl dressed as a balle-rina. She inhaled the aroma and bit off the head.

"The horror," yelped Tom. Taken aback, Lola's eyes grew wide and she quickly said, "What?" Tom was shaking his head in disbelief. "Only sadists start with the head. It's just not done," he said, biting off the foot from his soccer player in a demonstration. Lola scoffed at this and kept nibbling at her cookie as she dragged Tom from cart to cart to try everything they offered. Stuffed, they headed towards the line for sleigh rides and bumped into Clara and Gunther.

"Isn't it amazing? Do they do this every summer?" asked Lola.

"No, maybe every other summer. But it's always a treat," replied Gunther since Clara's mouth was full of roasted chestnuts.

Each couple had their own sled and they were far enough apart to offer a little privacy.

Their Latin teacher, Dr. Thompson, was overseeing the sleigh distribution. He beckoned Tom and Lola to get in and be seated. There was a fur throw and they pulled it up on their laps.

"Please remain seated and keep all body parts inside the sleigh at all times. Refrain from piercing shrieks as you may frighten the animals," he instructed. Then he patted the reindeer's rear and they were off. "Enjoy the ride!" he yelled after them with a wave.

"Animals?" blurted Lola.

"You'll see," replied Tom, reaching for her hand.

They started around the ice rink, around the hill, then into the forest. It really was an elaborate illusion. The ground was covered in snow and the sound all around them was muffled, as if the party they had just left was miles away. Lola was alert, looking here and there for foxes or deer to pop out at them. Tom nudged her and told her to relax. Nothing was going to jump out at them—it wasn't a haunted mansion. Lola made a sigh of relief and let her head drop onto Tom's shoulder. As she did, she looked up dreamily, expecting to see stars or snow falling. She sat up abruptly, slapping Tom's arms as she pointed a shaking finger up at the sky.

"It's an Aurora Borealis!" whispered Lola, reverently. "I've always wanted to see one," she said in a daze. Tom put an arm around her, tucked her into his side, and kissed the top of her head. Heads back, they took in the beauty of the sky for as long as it lasted. When the sky was dark again, Lola turned to face him. Tom shifted in the seat and looked deep into Lola's eyes. He cupped her face with a hand and caressed her face. Lola leaned into his hands and closed her eyes. He brought his face within an inch of hers and waited. She opened her eyes, sensing his closeness. They hung there, breathing each other's air for one, two, three heartbeats until their lips joined and breached the divide. It was a light, sweet kiss, full of hope, and promise. They pulled back, opened their eyes, and kissed again. This kiss lasted longer, was firmer, and as their lips parted and their tongues touched for the first time, they heard bells. No, not bells, whistles.

Lola cracked open an eye and drew back with a gasp. On their right, behind a sheer glass or invisible wall, was a huge gray whale swimming alongside them. Then another. It was like they were under the arctic ocean. They could see the underside of ice banks. Soon, they were seeing seals and polar bears diving into the ocean. There was even a walrus.

"Oh my God!" whispered Lola, with reverence. "That's the most beautiful thing I've ever seen," she breathed. Tom was equally taken with the sight and they were silent as the sleigh kept going. Eventually, they left the ocean and were back in the woods. The sounds of the party were getting closer; the ride was about to end. Tom picked up Lola's hand and kissed it. She looked up at him adoringly and he leaned down for one last, lingering kiss.

When they got back, they headed for the ice rink. Lady Samsara was in her element. She looked like Elsa from Frozen with her long, flowing blue gown, a silver fur cape, and what looked like a crown made of ice.

"What size skates do you need?" she asked Lola and Tom, then pointed them to numbered benches around the rink. They went to their respective benches, grabbed a pair of skates, and laced them up. Lola was not a good skater. She took a few tentative steps onto the ice and stopped. She waved at Tom to come over to her.

"I might need a hand here," she said grabbing onto his arm when he arrived. "At home, there is a border around the rink you can hold onto," she said apologetically.

"Never fear, my lady. Your knight is here for you," said Tom as he took her arm with one hand and put his other arm around her so he could steady her. They skated a few turns and Lola managed to stay upright. In the center, a girl was skating beautifully and bending into a graceful arabesque. Lola squinted and was surprised to see it was Sara. Devlin skated up to her and expertly took hold of her and they skated in perfect unison, hip to hip, like Olympic champions.

"He definitely got all the talent in our family," said Lola, eyes following the pair around the rink in fascination.

"They're making us look bad," replied Tom, pretending to be miffed.

But as they looked around them, the rest of the students were adequate skaters, no more, no less. Devlin and Sara were the oddities, arresting as they were. Most had stopped to stare at the couple, and when they came to a stop, they were met with applause. Lola grudgingly joined in and tugged on Tom so they could skate over and congratulate them.

"Where did you learn to skate like that?" asked Lola, looking from one to the other.

They looked at each other and replied, "Lessons," at the same time. A more elaborate explanation would have to wait because the twinkle lights above the rink started to blink, and they all knew what that meant.

They head back to their benches to take off their skates and met up again near the middle doorway. Lola took one last look at herself in winter garb and watched it all disappear as they went through the doors. On the other side, Tom took her hand and they headed back to school.

It was a magical night. Literally. She didn't know how much magic or illusion was necessary to pull this off, but Lola would remember it for the rest of her life.

7

SATURDAY

On Saturday, both Lola and Devlin were relieved when no summons came from the Headmaster. In the morning, the gang split up and the boys played a round of W&W while the girls chilled out in their rooms. In the afternoon, the boys played sports, and the girls lounged in the sun.

"Is this what we'll do every Saturday when we come back in the fall?" asked Lola.

Sara rolled onto her front and turned her head to face Lola.

"I'm not sure. I doubt there will be BBQs every week, but I'm pretty sure the sports and lounging should be fairly recurring," she answered.

"My sister said there are field trips once a month, though she didn't say where. And we get to go home one weekend each month if we want to. Most students only go home once per semester and some simply for the holidays," replied Lenora.

"Do some students just stay here all year and never go home?" asked Lola in disbelief.

"Yes, of course. Not everyone comes from a good home," put in Clara.

"I admit life here is pretty comfortable. It might be better than whatever they've got going on at home," mused Lola.

"Think of Devlin. If he wasn't your long-lost brother, he would likely have moved in here for the year. What would have been the point of going home to an empty house?" said Sara.

"Speaking of which, how are things going on that front? I mean, the new family dynamics," inquired Lenora.

"Devlin and I have talked a little, but things haven't really changed between us. We were already kind of acting like brother and sister. I guess going home will be the true test. He and Phyllis hit it off, so that's good. Once he's had a chance to settle in, we'll get his stuff from Sweden. We'll have the next month to bond as a family before coming back here," explained Lola.

"That sounds great. I'm glad you found one another. Though I must have dreamed of being an only child a million times growing up, the truth is I'd be lost without my siblings and my family," said Lenora, turning onto her back and closing her eyes.

Sara leaned in closer to Lola and dropped her voice.

"What about Jackson?" she whispered.

"What about him?" asked Lola, whispering too.

"Won't he be jealous?" asked Sara.

"Why would he be jealous? We're not dating!" she replied.

"If you now have an older brother, and he's the heir, there is no need for you to marry. Plus, Devlin would eventually be tasked with taking over the family finances since he's already eighteen and about to become Custodian. Wouldn't that put Jackson out of a job?" said Sara.

"I see your point. Also, before I left, we decided to have the attorneys look for a new couple to become caretakers so Jackson would be free to focus on college. So either way, it looks like he's about to lose his job, but it won't be because he and I are getting married. Now I feel terrible, and I haven't even brought up Tom!" said Lola, putting her face in her hands.

"You definitely should not mention Tom unless things start getting serious and you decide to become exclusive. And since you're going home tomorrow and won't see Tom until his party in two weeks, it's a moot point," suggested Sara.

"I guess you're right; one problem at a time," breathed Lola.

"And none of this is YOUR problem. You're a minor and no longer the heir. Your job is to have fun, get to know your brother, enjoy your new aunt and your new home. Let the adults and the attorneys figure it out!" said Sara, pointedly.

"Yes. You're right. None of this is my fault. I didn't ask for any of it. I'll just focus on the positives: I have two new family members and I'm not alone," said Lola with an affirmative nod of the head.

"And, of course, you have a sassy bunch of new mates at school who've got your back," said Sara, a little louder as she extended her arm for a fist bump. Lola laughed and pounded her fist with hers and they both did the explosion fingers afterward, giggling.

Lenora and Clara lifted their heads when they heard the giggles and saw the tail end of the fistbump. Rolling their eyes, they went back to tanning.

Meanwhile, on the East Lawn, the red team was crushing the blue team in a spirited game of soccer. Doctor McClary and Doctor Thompson were each captaining a team and competition was fierce.

Tom, playing for the red team, was moving fluidly and trying to shake Gunther. He cut to the right and then quickly lunged left. The ball moved with him as though it was tethered to his feet. He drew his leg back and his foot connected with the ball seconds before Gunther's foot made contact. It flew across the grass and into the upper right corner of the net, just as Tom and Gunther fell in a heap. And that's all she wrote; the reds had won. His teammates, whooping and hollering, came at him and they fell into a group hug, jumping in victory. Doctor McClary joined them and yelled, "Sodas are on me!" And the team, composed of boys and girls, cheered some more. He had them line up to shake hands with the other team and he led by example, shaking Doctor Thompson's hand first.

"Well played!" Doctor Thompson told each of them as they passed and they all gathered around a couple of coolers filled with chilled soda cans. They sat around, rehashing the game, doing play-by-plays of the best goals, and just relaxed after a fun game. When the chime sounded, Doctor McClary shouted, "Time to hit the showers, see you at dinner!"

8

LEAVING

On Sunday morning, Tom and Lola had breakfast together and headed out for one last stroll. It was still early and they were alone on the path. They held hands and talked about their summer plans. Tom said he was probably going to choose Liberal Arts as his major since he didn't really know what he wanted to do yet. He was excited that he and Lola were likely to have most of their classes together in the fall since they were both finishing high school.

"I wonder how many other students are in the same situation," Lola wondered.

"I'm sure we're not the only ones," said Tom, unsure.

"Technically, I shouldn't be coming back next year," said Lola.

"What do you mean?" asked Tom

"Now that we know Devlin is my brother, I'm no longer up for Custodian and could complete my studies back home and come back the following year," she said.

"And that's not what's going to happen?" he asked, worried now.

"No, the Headmaster said once we've received our letter of admission, it can't be revoked. I could choose not to come, but I obviously won't," said Lola, smiling shyly and nudging him with a shoulder. "I've grown fond of the school," she said coyly.

"Only the school?" he asked, cocking an eyebrow.

"Well, I've got all the new amazing friends too," she hedged.

"Anything else?" he urged.

"The food is amazing, and you've got to admit early morning flying with Professor Elderberry is the best," she replied, tongue in cheek.

Tom abruptly stopped walking and their hands unclasped as Lola kept going. She turned, arm outstretched, looking in confusion at where their hands had detached. She looked up at his face and saw the frown. She smiled and walked back to him, grabbed both his hands, and looked up earnestly at him, trying to coax a smile from him. His expression wouldn't budge. She released his hands and put them on his chest for balance and rose on tiptoe to kiss him lightly. Nothing. She pressed a little more, lingering a little longer, and felt him yielding. "Do I have to come out and say it?" she asked, her lips still pressed against his. His mouth twitched and he closed his lips together to suppress a smile. She took a step back and gave him a scrutinizing look. She was debating giving in to this obvious play for attention or letting him cool his heels. In the end, she just wasn't sophisticated enough for any kind of game and gave in.

"You, Tom, are one of the reasons why I am counting the days until we are back on campus," she said, honestly.

A slow smile crept up his face and he took a step closer to her. Close, but not touching. His eyes bore into hers, intense, but still dancing in amusement. He brought his hands up along her arms, not touching them. Lola shivered in anticipation. They settled on her face, caressing her cheeks with his thumbs.

"I like it when you're sassy, but don't get too cheeky. I also like that you are guileless and don't play games," he said quietly and she smiled. "I like everything about you, Lola Evers," he added, bending down to brush his lips against hers once, twice, three times. She closed her eyes to savor the feeling. He dropped butterfly kisses on her cheek, her temple, her forehead, and finally on her nose. When she opened her eyes, her heart was pounding, and he was smiling sweetly at her. She put her hand against his heart and could feel his heart was beating as rapidly as hers. Eyes locked on hers, one of his hands left her face and covered her hand. His other hand pushed her hair back behind her ear then slid down her back and he nudged her closer to him until her head was in the crook of his neck and he held her tight.

They embraced for a few minutes and then pulled apart. It was time to go. Hand in hand, they headed back to school and agreed to keep in touch once they were back at home. They would likely not see each other before Tom's party because he and his family were leaving on holiday for the next two weeks.

They parted in front of the dorm with a quick kiss and another long hug.

Lola went back to the room and started packing up her things. Sara was up and doing the same. As she was packing up her books, she thought about the Archives. She had no idea when the book had gone back to the attorney's vault. Only that when the Headmaster had asked to see it, it was gone. Lola was running a handful of options in her head. *Did it go back as soon as I arrived? Maybe it never left the Mansion and disappeared as soon as I crossed the door. Or perhaps it disappeared as soon as I met Devlin.* The book should have gone to him. Then again, the attorney had brought Lola the book. It had not appeared to her personally, so it made sense that the book should leave Lola and go back to the attorneys. This was one of the many discussions they needed to have when she and Devlin got home.

"Don't forget to give me your mobile number and your email," reminded Sara from across the room.

Lola went to the desk and got a piece of paper. On it, she also wrote her address in case Sara needed it to send a letter or to come for a visit. She gave it to Sara, who swapped it with her own information.

"I'd love for you to come to stay with us for a couple of days," said Sara.

"I'd like that too, and obviously if you came to our house, you'd also see Devlin," responded Lola with a wink.

"That *would* be amazing. But girl time is very important too," replied Sara seriously.

"I agree. Let me get settled back home and get back to you on dates," replied Lola.

The girls were all packed and ready to go. They hugged and promised to text as soon as possible.

"*Um*, Sara," asked Lola.

"What?"

"How do we send our trunk home if we can't open a door in our room? It's much too heavy for me to lift," said Lola, a frown appearing on her forehead.

"Oh, of course. Leave it there, at the foot of your bed. Someone will send it home later tonight," replied Sara.

"How?" asked Lola, still confused.

"I have no idea," replied Sara. "There's a chime, like someone ringing your doorbell, and the trunk appears on your front doorstep."

"Just like magic," whispered Lola, amazed.

"Exactly!" responded Sara, cheerily. "Are you ready? Shall we go down and say goodbye to everyone else?"

Lola nodded, grabbed her satchel, and they were out the door.

In the Main Hall, the older students were saying goodbye, hugging, and promising to see each other soon. Sara and Devlin grabbed each other's hands and whispered their goodbyes while Lola beamed at them.

Lola and Devlin then retrieved their information packets. When it was their turn to summon their door, Lola took out her key and thought Home. As the door appeared, she turned to Devlin and asked if he was ready for his new life. Devlin took a deep breath, straightened up, and followed her through the door.

9
HOME

They arrived at the end of the lane leading to the Evers Mansion. Lola wanted Devlin to get the full effect, so she tweaked their destination. Devlin did not disappoint. He stood there on the tree-lined gravel path, staring first at the fountain, then the Mansion. His jaw hung and he stared at Lola.

"This is our home?" he asked, disbelief written all over his face.

"Yes! Isn't it beautiful?" replied Lola, eyes bright with appreciation.

"It is spectacular!" replied Devlin.

Lola grabbed his hand and pulled him down the lane, pointing this way and that towards the garage, the pool, the gazebo, and the path that led into the woods. They went around the fountain and Devlin reached down to touch the water as they passed. Finally, they arrived in front of the Mansion, at the bottom of the steps.

"Ready?" she asked.

"Ready!" he answered.

They walked up the step and, on impulse, Lola decided to ring the doorbell. They waited.

Phyllis opened the door, and then wiped her hands on her apron, looking a little distracted, but with her gracious smile in place to greet whoever was at the door. Her face registered surprise and then was completely transformed by a genuine smile.

"Children! You're home!" she exclaimed and flung her arms around both of them.

"What on earth are you doing out here?" she asked, teary-eyed, as she let them go and ushered them inside.

"I wanted Devlin to see the house just like I did for the first time," replied Lola.

"Aren't you thoughtful," replied Phyllis. "Come on into the kitchen, lunch is almost ready," she said, heading in that direction.

Once in the kitchen, Devlin asked, "Can we help?"

"Thanks, sugar, you and Lola can go set the table out on the patio," replied Phyllis.

The plates, glasses, and cutlery were on the counter. They picked them up, brought them outside, and when they came back, found that Phyllis had set a pitcher of sweet tea and a platter of crudités on the counter. They brought those to the table too. Back in the kitchen, Phyllis was washing her hands and all three plates were ready on the counter. They were filled with BLTs and potato salad. Between them, they took the plates and went and sat down.

"Is Jackson out of town?" Lola asked, filling her glass with sweet tea.

"He's out with some friends. He'll be back in time to join us for dinner," replied Phyllis. "That should give Devlin time to get settled and have a bit of a tour."

Phyllis asked how their week had gone and they told her about their classes and the Winter Wonderland social on Friday as well as movie night on Saturday.

When lunch was finished, they washed and dried the dishes together and did a quick tour of the first floor before heading upstairs. Again, the tour was brief. Phyllis pointed to various rooms without opening them and said they could explore on their own. She led them to the room next to Lola's—the one Jane had used when she was here the last time. When Phyllis opened the door, Lola saw there was a new bedspread, curtains, and seat cushions on the window seat. The green hues added a more masculine feel to the red and gold room.

"I hope you like it," said Phyllis as they followed her in.

Devlin looked like he was in shock. He had worn the same expression throughout the tour, but the expression on his face now overrode even that.

"This room is almost bigger than the second floor of our townhouse!" Devlin replied, turning to take in his new room. "It is lovely, thank you, aunt Phyllis."

"Just call me Phyllis," she replied, giving him a peck on the cheek. "I'm glad you like it. I'm sorry it's not as large as the other rooms," she added.

Devlin looked at Lola and said, "Your room is bigger than this?" with an incredulous look on his face. Lola blushed and shrugged.

Checking her watch, Phyllis made to leave and announced, "It's almost two p.m. I'll let Lola show you her room and, if you like, you can peak into my room and Simon's room. I'm going to spend the afternoon with Boris. I'll be back in time for dinner." She kissed each of their cheeks and left.

"What do you want to do first?" asked Lola. "You can take a shower, or get some rest. We could finish the tour. We could go for a swim . . ." Lola suggested.

"What time is dinner?" asked Devlin.

"Six-thirty, sharp. And we dress for dinner," said Lola. She walked over to the closet and checked inside. Sure enough, there was a suit, three dress shirts, and two pairs of dress pants. Opening a drawer, she saw a couple of ties, dress and casual socks, boxer shorts, and a pair of pajamas. In another drawer, there was a pair of jeans and two t-shirts. Devlin peeked over her shoulder at the content in amazement.

"That should hold you over until your trunk gets here and you can get your other clothes from home. How did she know what size to get?" Lola wondered.

"She asked my permission to get a copy of the sizing sheet from school," replied Devlin, blushing as he pulled out a pair of boxer shorts.

"Don't worry about it, she did the same for me. She probably considers this emergency clothing and will take you shopping later," said Lola.

They closed the drawers and the closet and went to check out the bathroom. There was a full set of toiletries, a robe, and a pair of slippers.

"So, what will it be?" asked Lola.

"I would like to see your room and our father's room," replied Devlin.

They started with Lola's room and Devlin was impressed. When Lola apologized again about having a bigger room, he waved her away.

"My room is huge. If I need more space, I can always go to the Study," he said. "There are only three of us living here, we cannot possibly occupy all the space," he added.

Next, they went to the Gym. Lola explained their daily meditation and yoga ritual, and Devlin was pleased. He also seemed very impressed with the machines. They went next to the Nursery and Devlin flipped out; the same way Lola had.

"Can we sleep here tonight?" he asked, grinning like a kid.

"Sure, if you want," replied Lola. "I stayed in here a couple of times when my friend Jane came to visit," she added.

Lola took him to see the two other bedrooms. "There are smaller than your room, but if you prefer either of these, I'm sure Phyllis will let you switch," suggested Lola. But Devlin shook his head no, and they moved on to Phyllis' room. They knocked first and waited. Then, finding the door unlocked, they slipped in for a quick peek. Lola explained about Phyllis' extensive Traveling and her epilepsy.

"It looks like the cave of wonders!" exclaimed Devlin, shaking his head in amazement.

They left Phyllis' room and went to Simon's. Out of habit, and perhaps because of a bit of wishful thinking, Lola knocked on the door. There was no answer and they slipped inside. The room was unchanged from when Lola had last been here. Before heading up to the alcove, Lola showed Devlin the family Bible that Simon kept in his bedside table. Taking a pen she found in the drawer, Lola added Devlin's name next to her own.

"You're officially part of the family," she said handing him the book. He took it reverently and looked at all the names of their ancestors in awe. Lola grabbed his hand and led him up to the alcove. He was still clutching the Bible.

When his head cleared the top of the spiral staircase and he saw all the paintings, Devlin said something in Swedish, "*Herregud.*"

Lola asked him what he said and he said it meant *Oh My God.* Devlin flipped through the canvases stacked against the wall. When he found the portrait of Lola, he turned to her questioningly.

"He did it while he was here, Traveling from the past. I'm supposed to put it somewhere inconspicuous, but I haven't had a chance," said Lola. Then, remembering the time she spent with her father, and realizing Devlin would never get that chance, Lola started to cry.

Devlin walked over to her and wrapped her in a bear hug. "What is the matter, Lola?" he asked, rubbing her back soothingly.

"I'm so sorry you didn't get to meet him. It seems so unfair," she blubbered into his shirt.

"I am too, but I am so very happy to have found a family. You and Phyllis are here now. I can spend time with you and you can tell me about my father," he replied, seemingly not distressed.

Lola stepped away from him and wiped the tears from her eyes with the back of her sleeve. Turning, she reached for a tissue and blew her nose.

"I come here to feel closer to him. You can come here too, anytime," she said, taking a deep breath.

Then went back down to the room and Devlin put the Bible back in the bedside table. They left Simon's room and Lola explained about the attic.

"But really, now that we know how to Travel, we can just leave from our own rooms and come back there the way Phyllis does. When Marie, the cook/housekeeper is here during the week, Phyllis usually says she's resting in her room, locks the door and no one disturbs her. That should work for us too," explained Lola.

"Or we could say we are studying, or reading," ventured Devlin and Lola nodded.

"Does Jackson know? About the Traveling?" asked Devlin.

"Yes, he has a general idea," replied Lola.

Devlin checked his watch. It was two-forty-five.

"Lola, I know Phyllis said we would go to my house this week to pack up my things, but do you think you and I could go over now to pick up some stuff?" he asked.

Lola was surprised and thought about it before replying, "Sure, why not. Let's go back to your room."

IO

BREAK-IN

They went back to Devlin's room and he took out his key. The red door appeared. Lola told him to relax, take a deep breath and clearly picture the room in the house where he wanted to go and then think *Home* or, if that was too confusing because of his new home, to just say the address in his mind.

Devlin was about to reach out and turn the handle when he remembered the incantation for a window in the door, so he could make sure he was going to the right place. He peeked through, as did Lola.

"I hadn't pegged you for a messy person," chuckled Lola, upon seeing the state of his room.

Devlin's face was ashen. "I keep a very clean room," he responded through gritted teeth. "Something is very wrong," he added, his hand hovering over the handle.

"What do you mean?" asked Lola, a worried expression settling on her face.

"I think someone has burgled my house!" exclaimed Devlin, angry now as he turned the handle and barged in.

Lola was about to tell him to wait, but she wasn't fast enough. She hesitated on the sill and then decided to go with it. She went through and closed the door. It disappeared.

The room had been ransacked. Devlin, his face a mask of utter dismay, was picking up clothing, books, and various other objects in a vain attempt at putting things right.

"Maybe we shouldn't touch anything and call the police. They might need to dust for fingerprints," suggested Lola, hovering behind Devlin in case the intruders were still around.

"Yes, you are right. Though I doubt my fingerprints will be a problem. You had better keep your hands in your pockets," he suggested.

They left his room and went into the kitchen, then the living room, his mother's room, and the bathroom. Everything was topsy turvy.

Back in the living room, Devlin reached for the phone and was about to dial 112.

"Wait," she said and he put the receiver down.

"You do not think I should call the police?" asked Devlin.

"I think we should call Phyllis. I know this is your home and you're eighteen, but I have a really bad feeling about this," said Lola, wringing her hands. Devlin nodded, deciding to humor her. Lola took out her cell phone and texted Phyllis to meet them in Devlin's room in the Mansion and text her back when she was there. When her phone beeped, Devlin took out his key and opened a door to his room and let Phyllis through.

"Oh my Lord, what happened here?" she breathed.

"Someone broke in," said Devlin, stating the obvious.

"Was anything taken?" asked Phyllis and Devlin shook his head no but added, "Not that I can see."

"Are you sure they've gone?" she inquired. When both Lola and Devlin nodded, she asked her final question, "Are there signs of a break-in? Broken window, forced lock?"

"I did not notice any up here. Let's go downstairs," he said and walked to a door Lola hadn't noticed. It opened to a flight of stairs and they went down.

On the first floor, there was the main door that led to the street, one door leading to a utility room, and another door leading to the single-car garage. The main door looked intact. Nothing in the utility room appeared to be disturbed. When they checked the garage, the small VW Polo was where it should be.

Heading back upstairs, they went from room to room, checking windows and doors for signs of a break-in. When they checked in his mother's room, Phyllis stopped in the middle of the room, sniffing the air. "Devlin, did your mother have a boyfriend?" she asked, turning towards him.

Devlin made a face and laughed. "No, mother did not have a boyfriend. As far as I know, my mother has not dated anyone in the last decade!" he exclaimed. "Why do you ask?"

"I have a very good nose and I smell a man's aftershave. Could it be yours?" she asked.

"I do not wear aftershave. As you can see, I do not have much of a beard," he replied.

Phyllis was frowning. "It's a familiar scent. A little woodsy," she said and she closed her eyes in concentration and sniffed the air some more. Lola and Devlin just stared at her.

She looks like a hound dog looking for clues, thought Lola.

"What was that?" he asked Lola, eyes huge, grabbing her shoulders.

She stared at him in bewilderment. He closed his eyes and tried to send her a message through telepathy. *That is not a very polite thing to say about Phyllis.* Lola's eyes nearly bulged out of her head. *I didn't say that out loud. Did you just read my thoughts?*

When Devlin replied, "Yes!", Lola's jaw dropped. She was about to say something about it when Phyllis' eyes flew open and she grabbed Lola's arm.

"Donatelli!" she screamed.

At first, Lola didn't place the name. Then she remembered—the kidnapping.

"Who is Donatelli?" asked Devlin.

Phyllis had turned white and was now shaking visibly. Devlin led her out of the room and into the living room, where he gently urged her onto the sofa. He turned an inquisitive look on Lola.

Donatelli is the name of the man who kidnapped her in Florence, thought Lola.

Devlin's face scrunched up in confusion. *Kidnapped? I will need details, later. What should we do?* he thought, warming up to this new way of communicating with Lola. Lola shrugged and turned to Phyllis.

"Phyllis?" she asked, gently putting a hand on her aunt's shoulder. "Are you alright? Should we call Boris?"

At the mention of Boris, Phyllis seemed to snap out of it. "Boris! Yes, Boris will know what to do," she said, her confidence coming back. She rose and looked at Devlin.

"Call your attorney and tell him what happened. Since there are no damages and nothing was stolen, I don't think we need to call the police. A police report would be required for an insurance claim. And I can't imagine having to explain all this to the police," said Phyllis with a lingering shudder. Phyllis took out her phone and dialed Boris' office and was patched through immediately. She summarized the situation.

Devlin went to his room to call his attorney to update him on the break-in and request that he start proceedings to sell the Townhouse and the car. They would hire a cleaning crew after he had packed the things he wanted to take to his new home. He briefly explained about his new family. At one point, he came out to ask Phyllis the name of their attorney as well as their home address and phone number. While she had him there, Phyllis asked for his Townhouse address to give to Boris. Devlin provided the information to his attorney and hung up.

Meanwhile, Phyllis had given Boris the address, and within minutes he was ringing the doorbell to the Townhouse. Devlin went down to let him in.

"It's a pleasure to meet you, young man. I wish it had been under more pleasant circumstances. Could you give me a tour so I can check the doors and windows? Perhaps I might notice something you and the others did not," said Boris.

"Yes, sir. It would be my pleasure. Let's start downstairs," replied Devlin, and Boris followed him to the garage. After touring the lower floor, they headed upstairs.

Meanwhile, Lola went to the kitchen and made tea. That always helped Phyllis to relax and she needed to do something. She rummaged in the kitchen and found tea bags and cups. The kettle was on the stove. When she couldn't find a tray, she put cups with some sugar and a spoon on a cutting board and set it on the coffee table. Phyllis took one of the cups gratefully. Lola wasn't much of a tea drinker, but she figured it couldn't hurt and holding the cup would give her something to do.

When the men came up the stairs, Devlin took Boris room to room, then came to sit with the ladies in the living room. Boris took a cup of tea, but Devlin refused.

"The intruder either had a key to your Townhouse or it was a magical break-in. Phyllis thinks it might be the same man who abducted her last month, but I found no other evidence than the lingering scent. Someone was here and made a mess trying to find something. Do you know what it could be?" asked Boris.

"We don't have anything of value," replied Devlin, completely baffled. They were all stumped.

"Everything is secure now. Devlin has spoken to his attorney. I think we can leave, there's nothing more to be done here," stated Boris.

"Let me get my phone and charger, and pack a bag of essentials," said Devlin, heading into his room.

As Devlin rummaged through the mess looking for his things, Lola shared her concerns about a magical break-in with the others

"The Traveling Handbook says you can't Travel into another person's home. You always arrive outside," said Lola.

"You're right," replied Boris. "But it could be another type of magical break-in."

"What do you mean?" asked Phyllis.

"A Traveler did not open a door into the Townhouse. But that does not mean he, or an accomplice, did not use a spell to open the door once they arrived outside," he replied.

"I hadn't thought of that," said Lola. "By an accomplice, you mean another Traveler?"

"No, I mean a witch or a wizard. I don't think they teach this kind of incantation at The Academy," said Boris gravely.

Devlin came out of his room with a small duffle bag. On impulse, Devlin grabbed a piece of paper and a pen and started writing what looked like a letter.

"Who are you writing to?" asked Lola, peering over his shoulder. He didn't need to respond because she saw he was writing to the Headmaster.

"I think we should let him know about the break-in, in case it had any bearing on his ongoing investigation." He also told him about the telepathy incident and let him know he would be living at the Evers Mansion from now on. He folded the letter the way they were taught, addressed it to *Headmaster Lianon, The Academy* and they waited for it to disappear.

"I'm ready to go home now," said Devlin, dropping the pen and getting up. He grabbed his duffel bag and nodded to his new family.

When they all looked at each other wondering who would do the honors, Lola fished out her key from around her neck and her door appeared. It felt awkward to take them to her room, and she didn't want to come face to face with Marie or Jackson by going to the Library, so she took them to the School Room. From there, Boris and Phyllis went to her room to chat before Boris went back to work. Phyllis told them she would see them at dinner.

I I

BOYS

I t felt like they'd been gone for hours, but it was only four-thirty. There was plenty of time to shower and change for dinner.

"Do you want to go for a quick walk outside?" asked Lola.

"Yes, I think that would help clear my head," replied Devlin.

Lola grabbed her cell and her house keys. They went down and out through the mudroom. Lola explained how the house keys, the chip, and the security system worked, saying he would probably get his own keys later in the week.

They bypassed the garage since neither was ready to face Jackson. Though Lola had missed him, her thoughts were too unsettled at present for their reunion to be comfortable.

They headed for the path and stopped by the gazebo, the pool and pool house, Phyllis' garden, and the Guest House. Lola explained that was where the next housekeeper and groundskeeper would live.

"It is a very cozy and welcoming house. Does Jackson not live here?" he asked, noticing the sheets on the furniture to keep away dust.

"No, he has an apartment over the garage," replied Lola.

"Have you been inside?" asked Devlin, pointedly.

Lola blushed and nodded. Wanting to change the subject, they left the house and headed for the wooded area.

As they neared the midpoint, Lola told him that was the spot where her father had appeared to her for the first time and how she had fainted.

"I think that's when the fainting episodes started, actually," she said with a laugh.

Devlin asked her to tell him everything she remembered about the time she spent with their father.

She told him about studying the Archives, about the kidnapping, the Council, and finally her birthday party.

"It was quite a hectic time for you," Devlin said.

"Yes, it was," replied Lola.

They fell silent and they kept walking.

"So what's up with the telepathy?" asked Lola, suddenly remembering what had happened at the Townhouse.

"I don't know!" exclaimed Devlin. "When I was in the Headmaster's office once, he said I had a predisposition to it."

"Me too!" said Lola.

They discussed it as they walked and practiced doing it again in case it had been a fluke. But it wasn't. Soon they were back on the lawns and they headed back to the house but entered through the sliding doors of the patio.

The tantalizing aroma of sizzling garlic led them to the kitchen where Phyllis was making dinner. Spotting them, she smiled.

"What's for dinner?" asked Lola.

"Pecan-crusted pork tenderloin with pineapple and mango chutney served with a green salad," she replied.

"That sounds delicious!" exclaimed Devlin, eyes lighting up at the prospect.

"With pecan pie for dessert!" added Phyllis, smiling proudly and nodding at the oven.

Both Lola and Devlin replied, "My favorite!" at the same time. They looked at each other and burst out laughing.

"I know," replied Phyllis, a contented smile on her face. "Now run along and get changed. We have a lot to talk about," said Phyllis, shooing them out of the kitchen.

Just before leaving the kitchen, Lola replied, "You have no idea!"

Lola was putting in her earrings when there was a knock at the door. Thinking it was Devlin, probably nervous about going down by himself, she bellowed, "Come in!" She checked her appearance one last time and headed for her sitting room. She stopped short, mouth open.

It wasn't Devlin, it was Jackson. He was standing by the door, hands clasped behind his back, waiting for her.

"Jackson," she breathed.

"Lola," he replied softly.

Their eyes locked and Lola felt drawn to him. Her feet started pulling her towards him and only stopped when she was inches away.

"I missed you," he said, his minty breath a cool balm on her heated cheeks.

"Me too," she said sincerely. He was so handsome in his gray dress pants and pale lavender shirt. Lola eyed the bare skin at the base of his throat where his shirt was open. Her lips parted and her eyes drifted up to meet his. He bent down and touched his lips to her forehead, softly. Then, he wrapped her in a warm hug and said, "Welcome home."

There was another knock at the door. The knocker didn't wait for an answer and came right in.

"Oh, sorry," said Devlin, though he did not look sorry. "Am I interrupting?" he asked cheerfully.

"Not at all," drawled Jackson, keeping his hold on Lola. Lola extricated herself and gave him a look that said *What's wrong with you?* She stepped closer to Devlin.

"Devlin, may I introduce Jackson, a good friend of the family," she said. "And Jackson, this is Devlin, my brother," she said, beaming.

"It is nice to meet you," said Devlin. He held out his hand to Jackson, who shook it.

"Alleged half-brother," replied Jackson. "Likewise, I'm sure."

The tension was palpable and it was making Lola uncomfortable.

But she preferred they had it out here, instead of downstairs in front of Phyllis.

"It's not quite time to go down, Devlin. Did you need something?" asked Lola.

"Lola, this shirt has no buttons at the sleeves," he said, pointing to the right wrist.

"Ah, yes. I believe you're meant to put cufflinks in. Check the drawer that has the ties," she said. Then, looking at his bewildered expression, she added, "I'll come help you. Would you give me a moment with Jackson?"

"I do not think it is appropriate for Jackson to be alone with you in your room," he exclaimed. Lola made a face and said in her mind *Don't start that again!* He opened the door and waited out in the hall for her but he did not close the door.

"Jackson, you go down. I'll help Devlin and we'll be there soon," she said. She placed a hand on his arm and added, "We'll get a chance to talk more, later."

He kissed her cheek and left the room, nodding stiffly at Devlin on his way out.

Lola took a deep breath, straightened her shoulders, and followed Devlin back to his room. They found gold cufflinks in a small drawer they had missed. It also held what looked like Simon's watch. Neither the watch nor the cufflinks looked new.

Reverently, Devlin removed his sports watch and put on Simon's watch. Then Lola helped him with the cufflinks.

"How do I look?" he asked, taking a spin. He was wearing dress pants in a rather bold blue hue and a pale blue shirt, open at the collar like Jackson's.

"Perfect!" exclaimed Lola. Checking her own watch, she urged him towards the door. It would never do to be late.

They had drinks on the covered porch and, other than a few awkward moments between Devlin and Jackson, things went well.

Once seated at the dinner table, their conversation revolved mostly around their two weeks at the Academy. Jackson had little of interest to tell and Phyllis shared that she had spent most of her time with Boris.

Jackson did not broach the topic of Devlin's sudden appearance and Phyllis did not mention anything about the Council or her talks with the Headmaster. There was obviously no talk of Tom, and neither Lola nor Devlin spoke about their new telepathy abilities.

Basically, it was a typical family Sunday dinner where everyone made small talk and swept everything else under the rug.

After dinner, Jackson asked Lola if she would join him for a walk. Lola demurred, saying she was tired and was looking forward to sleeping in her own bed.

Once he had left, Phyllis said she was headed for the Library and was about to bid them goodnight when Lola said she and Devlin would join her for a little while, if she didn't mind. Curious, Phyllis smiled mischievously and headed for the Library.

"Phyllis has brandy and reads in the Library every night," explained Lola when they arrived.

Devlin nodded appreciatively. "Would you like one?" asked Phyllis, holding the bottle out to him.

"No, thank you," replied Devlin, politely.

Phyllis poured one for herself and went to sit at the desk, gesturing for them to sit in the armchairs. "Alright, what is it?" asked Phyllis, lighting a cigar. "I could tell there was something on your mind at dinner," she said as she blew out smoke and put her feet up on the desk.

Lola and Devlin looked at each other, but neither said anything.

"If it's about the Keys, and Archives, and that Headmaster of yours, I'm afraid it's much too late to have that discussion. Perhaps we can postpone it until tomorrow?" she suggested.

"Yes. I mean, no. We can talk about that and other things tomorrow," said Lola.

"Lola and I can communicate telepathically," blurted Devlin.

Phyllis nearly choked on her brandy. Her feet dropped on the floor and her head shot up. "Say that again, sugar?" she choked out.

And so they explained how the Headmaster had tested them both individually but hadn't told either of them so they hadn't discussed it. She was nodding now, as though agreeing with them.

"It was like that between Simon and I. We didn't communicate as you do, but we always knew what the other was thinking, or sometimes feeling. We had a bond. I'm thinking this is a more developed version of that," she mused.

"Anything else?" she asked, getting up and coming towards them. They shook their heads and got up too.

She embraced each of them and said goodnight. She invited them to join her for meditation and yoga the following morning.

Lola and Devlin nodded and left Phyllis to her nightly ritual.

As they reached the stairs, they noticed their trunks had arrived in the foyer. Neither felt like hefting the trunks up that night, so they just left them there. Devlin suggested they find a way to bring them up with their keys and Lola laughed but agreed. Devlin opened his trunk and grabbed a few personal items and they headed upstairs.

"Devlin, do you mind if we sleep in our respective rooms tonight? I really am tired," said Lola. "I know it's your first night . . ." she trailed.

"Do not worry about me. Tonight, I sleep in a room with a bed fit for a king. I shall sleep like royalty!" he replied, spreading his arms wide on each side. Lola laughed.

Lola hugged him goodnight and slipped into her room.

12

QUIET

Devlin woke up in a state of hypervigilance. He sat up abruptly and looked around him, searching for whatever had woken him. He hadn't set an alarm and the room was silent, empty. He leaned back on the pillows and tried to recall what he had been dreaming about, but he just couldn't remember. He felt alert, but not anxious or frightened. Perhaps he had simply slept very well and was extremely refreshed.

He checked his watch and saw it was already seven-thirty. He remembered going to bed at nine-thirty the night before, exhausted. He couldn't remember the last time he got a solid ten hours of sleep. He felt good.

What time did Phyllis say she did her morning meditation? He thought it was eight. Looking out the window, he saw it was sunny, which meant she would be in the Gazebo. He got up, made his bed, and went to the bathroom. He brushed his teeth, grabbed a pair of shorts and a t-shirt from his duffel, and shoved his feet into his leather sandals.

Out in the hall, he paused in front of Lola's room, debating whether to knock or not. Lola had said she was very tired, perhaps she planned to sleep in. He kept on going and went to join Phyllis in the Gazebo.

She was setting up three yoga mats and three meditation cushions.

"Good morning," boomed Devlin.

Phyllis gave a start, dropped a cushion and her right hand flew to her heart.

"Now, sugar, you have to learn not to creep up on people like that," chided Phyllis, fanning herself with her hand.

Devlin's smiling face fell. "I apologize for frightening you. That is what I wanted to avoid by saying good morning," he said, looking pained.

"Don't be sorry, honey. I was inside my head and wouldn't have noticed a herd of elephants until they were right on top of me. I'm just being silly. Let me try that again," said Phyllis, recovering from her shock. "Good morning, Devlin. Did you sleep alright?" she cooed, beckoning him to come into the Gazebo.

Devlin hesitantly stepped forward and replied, "I slept like a king and woke up in a palace."

"I'm glad. Have you seen Lola?" she asked.

"I have not and dared not knock on her door in case she was sleeping in," he replied.

Phyllis checked her watch. It was seven-fifty, they still had a few minutes. She explained her routine to Devlin and he nodded. He told her about meditating with his mother before she had passed away.

"How are you doing? I'm assuming you had even less time to process everything than Lola did, what with the summons to the Academy," she asked.

"It was the best thing that could have happened to me. I might have dwelled on it too much, or floundered, not knowing what to do. I had just finished secondary school, with no plans for University because we could not afford it. I would eventually have had to look for a job," he replied. He saw Phyllis' focus change and turned to see Lola coming towards them in her pink pajamas and bunny slippers. He started laughing and she frowned.

"Are you laughing at me, first thing in the morning?" she asked, clearly pretending to be upset.

"I am sorry, Lola, but you look like a six-year-old," he said, covering his mouth with his hand to cover his mirth.

"And so it begins," said Phyllis ruefully. "You have just had your first taste of siblinghood. I believe it is the older brother's prerogative to tease his little sister," she added, clapping her hands in delight.

"Indeed," said Devlin, beaming proudly.

"Can we meditate now, or do you want to gang up on me some more?" asked Lola. "Need I remind everyone that I am not a morning person and this routine is usually done in complete silence and serenity," she exclaimed, anything but serene.

"Quite right. Let's begin," said Phyllis as she sat on her cushion and set the timer for twenty minutes.

Lola and Devlin sat on their respective cushions and relaxed into the meditation. When the timer went off, they discarded the cushions and Phyllis led them through a series of asanas for another twenty minutes.

Once that was done, Lola could see Devlin was about to resume talking non-stop. She put up a hand to stop him. She placed a finger on her lips and whispered, "No talking before coffee. See you at breakfast." She kept her hand in place to ensure he stayed put and walked back to the house.

Phyllis and Devlin waited until she had closed the sliding door before resuming their conversation.

"She definitely is not a morning person," stated Devlin and Phyllis burst out laughing.

"No, she really isn't. But you are, I'm happy to see," she said, bending to roll her yoga mat and putting it in one of the gazebo benches they used for storage. Devlin rolled Lola's mat and his own and picked up the three cushions to store them.

They walked back to the house, arm in arm, and chatted about nothing special.

Despite being very tired, Lola had not slept well, and being greeted by two chatty Cathies when she went down to meditate had not helped things. She should have gone to the Gym by herself. She had gotten used to her solo morning routine at the Academy.

She needed coffee, pronto. Instead of heading upstairs to shower and change for the day, she made a detour to the Sunroom where breakfast was laid out in the morning. She would just slip in, get a cup, and take it up to her room. But life was never that simple. Jackson was at the table, reading the newspaper. He looked up and smiled.

"Good morning, gorgeous!" he exclaimed.

Lola closed her eyes and sighed. "I just need a cup of coffee, then I'll be sociable. Okay?" she pleaded but didn't wait for a response. She made a beeline for the sideboard, grabbed a cup, poured coffee, splashed some cream, and dropped a sugar cube in. She took a long sip, topped up her cup, and mumbled "Later!" as she left the room post-haste.

She should have taken the whole carafe and locked herself in her room for the morning until her mood improved. But then, she'd die of starvation. Perhaps she could use her key, call a door to the Sunroom with a window, check to see if anyone was in there, load up her plate and go back to her room, with everyone none the wiser. She laughed to herself. *There, that wasn't so hard. Just think happy, or funny, thoughts!*

She wanted to stop and get her book out of her trunk on the way, but she was afraid Jackson might come that way on his way out. She would get it later. Besides, she had to write to Jane and tell her she was back from camp. She really had no idea what else she could tell her. She could tell her about Devlin. And she could tell her about Tom. That would be sufficient material for many conversions or email exchanges, whichever was more convenient.

Back in her room, Lola went directly to her alcove and sat in the chair to sip her coffee and look out the huge bay window. She took deep breaths and started to relax. Then she remembered her journal and took it out. She made a few test scratchings on a piece of paper with the ink and quill, then began to write in her best handwriting. She started by making a list of all the things she was grateful for in her life.

Coffee, delicious food, Phyllis, her father, Devlin, Jackson, Tom, Sara, her new friends at school, Traveling, the Mansion, the internet and electronics, Magic, kissing . . .

This last word sent her thoughts back to Jackson. And Tom. How could kissing both of them feel so good but yet feel so completely different? *Duh, because they are different people, genius!* It was true they were different, but the mechanics should have been the same. Two pairs of lips touching. Then again, the same could be said about hugging. Two warm bodies hugging felt good, but there was a huge difference between hugging a parent, a sibling, or even a friend and hugging someone you liked. Someone you were attracted to.

Lola sighed and put down her quill. Enough of that. She finished sipping her coffee in quiet contemplation. Checking the time, she quickly opened the laptop and checked her email.

Jane had replied to her brief email about leaving for camp. She had met a boy at work. His name was Mike and he was heading to Johns Hopkins to study Biochemical Engineering. They had gone on a couple of dates and things were going well.

Lola gave her a watered-down version of how she found out Devlin was her half-brother and a detailed account of the budding relation- ship with Tom. She also mentioned the heat between her and Jackson on the day she left for camp and their steamy reunion when she came back. Lola desperately wanted to know if this made her a harlot. Jane would know.

She sent off the email, then saw that Sara had written a quick hello to confirm her email address. Lola sent her a short response and closed the laptop.

She went back down to her room and headed for the bathroom to shower. She stayed under the spray for a long time, savoring the heat and the pounding of the jets on her neck and back. After her shower, she felt rejuvenated and ready to take on the world. She brushed out her hair and let it air-dry.

She padded into her walk-in closet and smiled. "I've missed you", she said to her beautiful clothes and tried to decide what to wear. She doubted they had any plans for the day, and it had been quite warm outside this morning. She chose a pretty sundress with yellow and purple flowers on it and slipped into a pair of white sandals. She added a small pair of gold hoop earrings to complete the ensemble. Nice enough for an outing if one was proposed, and casual enough to wear while lounging in the hammock with her book.

She hung her towel in the bathroom, retrieved her coffee cup, and headed down to breakfast. Lola 2.0.

13

ROUTINE

Lola breezed into the Sunroom with a smile on her face. She really did need to start the day with at least an hour to herself. Now that Devlin would be living here, Lola wouldn't feel guilty about not spending every waking moment with Phyllis. Ironically, she figured Phyllis would feel the same way: that Devlin and Lola could spend time together while she spent time with Boris. And Devlin, he was just happy to have a home and family. Lola was pretty sure he'd go along with just about anything.

"There's the Lola I remember! Good morning, darling!" said Phyllis, warmly.

"I have no idea what you're referring to," replied Lola, cheekily. She went over to Phyllis and placed a kiss on her cheek.

"I don't understand. You were always in a good mood in the morning at school; perhaps you have low blood sugar and eating turns you into a nicer person," said Devlin, so earnestly that Lola couldn't take offense.

"It's because I got up at the crack of dawn before any of the other girls were up. I would meditate, do some yoga, have one or two cups of coffee, and then go down to breakfast. It's not that I'm not a morning person, it's that I'm not a people person!" she chuckled, and Devlin nodded, as though filing away this information for later use.

He had already been to the sideboard and his plate was full. Lola brought her cup for a refill and placed it on the table then went back to fill her plate. She missed Marie's homemade muffins and preserves. She inhaled the fresh-baked goodness as she put it on her plate. She got a bowl and poured some Greek yogurt, then added some granola and some berries. *That would be a good start*, she thought and went to join the others.

"So what's on the agenda today, and for that matter, this week?" asked Lola, between mouthfuls of yogurt.

"I haven't accepted any invitations or extended any of my own before Friday, so you two could get settled. However, Mr. Radcliff, our attorney, will be joining us for dinner tonight. He has a few topics to discuss with us and, from what you told me last night, it seems we might have a few to discuss with him as well," she said. "So let's save those sensitive topics for tonight," she added.

"Once we've settled everything, we'll make plans to move you in properly, Devlin. But I assume you have what you need for now?" she asked.

"Yes, I have everything that I need," he said. Then remembered there was something he wanted to ask about.

"Lola has told me that you do not drive, and she does not yet have a license," he started. "I have looked it up on the internet, and my Swedish driver's license is valid for up to six months in Virginia. After that, I will need to apply for an American driver's license," he explained. "So we will not need to rely on Jackson all the time to chauffeur us. He can remain available for you, as it should be," he concluded.

"Oh, yes. I hadn't thought of that. It will be useful to have an extra driver on hand. Remind me to have you added to our insurance policy," said Phyllis, absently. "Until that's settled, you'll have to make do with Jackson if you want to go into town," she said.

"There is no hurry. I am quite content here getting to know such charming ladies," said Devlin with a completely guileless smile. Phyllis smiled and placed a hand on his.

"Let me just recap our house routine. I meditate and do yoga every morning at eight. You are free to join as often as you like, no need to let me know in advance.

"Marie arrives around seven-thirty and has breakfast set up in the Sunroom by eight. Jackson usually comes in for breakfast around eight-thirty or nine. I have breakfast at ten. There is no set time for lunch, nor is any food laid out, though the pantry is well stocked. If you want something special to be prepared, you need to let Marie know before nine. Ideally the night before. For example, if you want her to assemble a picnic basket, or prepare a cold lunch to take on a hike.

"She cleans the upper rooms from nine to eleven and takes care of the lower rooms and the laundry from eleven to one. Then she makes dinner and does any prep work required for the next day. She leaves at two-thirty.

"In the afternoon, I usually retire to my room and should not be disturbed. I'm either resting or Traveling. Dinner is at six-thirty sharp. Cocktails are at six, but are not mandatory unless we have guests," concluded Phyllis.

"Basically, we can do whatever we want so long as we are suitably attired and on time for dinner," chuckled Lola.

"Well, yes. Within reason, of course. As you are a minor, Lola, and I am ultimately responsible for you, I would prefer you not get into too much mischief," said Phyllis.

"Only a little mischief," said Lola with a wink.

"I am here now and can look out for my sister," said Devlin, with a confident nod.

Lola looked at him askance and sighed.

"Anyway. What are the proposed weekend plans?" asked Lola, changing the subject back to a more interesting topic.

"I've invited the Maxwells to dinner on Friday. You remember Matthew and Sheila?" Phyllis asked Lola.

"Yes, they're really nice. I think Sheila is nineteen and Matthew is seventeen. You'll like them," she said to Devlin, who only smiled and nodded.

"And Saturday?" asked Lola.

"We've been invited to a house party at the Compton's in Virginia Beach. They don't have children your age, but they've invited families who do, including the Maxwells. Do you think you'll be up for it?" asked Phyllis.

"What does a house party entail?" asked Devlin.

"Guests arrive any time after lunch on Saturday and leave after brunch on Sunday. It's only about an hour away, so we could come back whenever we wanted if we kept the car. Otherwise, Jackson would drop us off and pick us up again the next day," explained Phyllis.

"You had me at beach," exclaimed Lola, doing a little dance in her seat.

"It seems like fun. I would love to go," concurred Devlin, laughing at Lola.

"Wonderful! I'll confirm with Maisy. I had tentatively accepted and told her I wanted to check with you," replied Phyllis. Then, turning to Devlin, she asked, "Do you have a swimsuit?"

"Yes, I do," replied Devlin.

"If you need an extra one, there is a stack of new ones in various sizes in the pool house. We keep them on hand for guests. Just pick the one you like and it's yours! You'll find towels there as well. Though beach and pool towels are usually provided at house parties," explained Phyllis.

"What should we pack?" asked Lola.

"Dinner should be an outdoor BBQ. If you have a sundress that's a little dressier than that, it would be perfect. Bring pants and a sweater for after dark. It can get nippy. There should be a bonfire on the beach, and perhaps fireworks. For you, Devlin, a short-sleeved shirt and nice Bermudas for the BBQ. For brunch the next day, a garden party dress for you, Lola, and an outfit like you are wearing tonight for you, Devlin, though lighter colors," she said. Seeing their panicked faces, she added, "I'll come around your rooms on Thursday and if we need to go shopping, we'll go that afternoon."

With that, Phyllis got up, brought her dishes into the kitchen, and told them she'd be in the garden if they needed her.

Lola and Devlin finished breakfast and discussed their plans for the day.

"First thing on the agenda is to get our trunks into our rooms," said Devlin.

"Yes! Except it's best we wait until after Marie has gone for the day, unless we plan on carrying them. But I don't think that's what you meant," replied Lola.

"Oh, yes, I see," said Devlin, turning towards the kitchen but Marie wasn't in there.

"And she's probably up in our rooms now anyway. Do you want to go and get our swimsuits and head to the pool?" suggested Lola.

"Yes, good idea. They've kept us so busy the last two weeks that I feel restless," said Devlin.

"I know; me too! I think I'll bring a book to read if you don't mind," she said.

"I'll do the same," he replied.

They went up and said they would meet at the pool in fifteen to twenty minutes.

***

They were lounging by the pool, reading companionably under the shade of an umbrella. Devlin was even paler than Lola, so it was her turn to insist he put sunscreen on. They did each other's backs, which was only slightly awkward. Though they had immediately felt comfortable when they met, living together as brother and sister was a whole other level of intimacy that would take some getting used to.

The good news was that they had both been raised as an only child and were used to being on their own. They were both mature for their age, responsible, and self-sufficient to a point. Though Devlin was obviously a people person at any time of day, he wasn't going to be clingy. Lola thought he took the protective older brother thing a little too seriously, but she figured if roles had been reversed, she might have acted the same way. It must be fun to have a little brother or sister. As it was, they were only two years apart and had attended all the same classes at the Academy while they were there. So Lola saw Devlin as her age. However, those two extra years might be packed with a lot of life experience. Not least of which was a driver's license.

"Did you have a girlfriend in Sweden?" asked Lola, seemingly out of nowhere.

Devlin, who had been engrossed in his book, lifted his head and said, "Excuse me?"

Lola repeated her question and he shook his head no. "Have you ever had a girlfriend? Who did you go to the prom with? Is there a prom at the end of high school?" asked Lola, sitting up straighter, her book forgotten on her lap.

Devlin bookmarked his page and put his book on the table between them. A smile crept up his face as he remembered.

"Yes, there is a prom in Sweden. I went with Astrid, a very pretty blonde girl. She was my girlfriend at the time, though not my first," he replied.

"What happened? Why did you break up? How long had you been dating?" asked Lola, her new questions coming out as rapid-fire as the first batch.

"We had been dating since starting upper secondary school. For you, that would be Juniors or two school years. She left the day after prom for Paris because she had a modeling contract. She was going to share a flat with other models," he said.

"You mean for the summer?" Lola asked.

"No, she moved there permanently. She has been modeling since she was fourteen and her parents insisted she finish her secondary education. So she would take contracts during summer vacation and other school holidays. Once she missed a whole month of school because she got a very small part in a film," he explained.

Lola got out her phone and said, "What's her name?"

"Astrid Berggren," replied Devlin, and Lola's fingers flew over the phone. Her jaw dropped and she flipped the phone over to validate she had the right girl. "Is this her?" she squealed. Devlin looked at the photo and gave a sad smile and a nod.

"Oh. My. God. You dated a supermodel!" she said, completely entranced as she scrolled through pic after pic on her phone. Then, realizing this might be painful for Devlin, she closed her phone and set it on the table.

"I'm sorry it didn't work out," she said sympathetically.

"We were never really in love. She was more of a best friend, and that's what I was sorry about when she left. But then I went to the Academy and met you, and Sara, and all our new friends. And here we are, lounging by the pool of our very own Mansion. I think I will survive," he said cheekily.

14

TRUNKS

They spent most of the day by the pool relaxing. Around noon, they got hungry and went to the kitchen to make some lunch and ate it on the patio. While inside, Devlin had grabbed his copy of the Traveling Handbook, and the Magic textbooks, hoping to find ways to move the trunk.

"You're very determined," said Lola with a laugh. "You realize we could have just brought the contents up one by one at least ten times since we've come home," she joked.

"It is the principle of it," he replied. "Besides, we need to practice. I'm sure our friends know how to do this and other practical things," he added.

"But can't we just call a door to our room, open it, and push the trunk in?" she asked.

Devlin looked at her dumbly and slapped his hand to his forehead. "You are correct. I have been overthinking this," he said, laughing at his own stupidity.

"That's one thing we have in common. I'm the Queen of Over-thinking," Lola said with a laugh. "But we can still practice the incantations we learned. And I'm pretty sure there are some in the book that we haven't used yet," she suggested.

"I was wondering how to move my things from the Townhouse. But it will be very simple; we just open a door and pass things through it as though it was a door to any other room in the same house," said Devlin and Lola nodded.

"Do you remember seeing anything about telepathic abilities in any of our books?" asked Lola, growing serious.

"No, I don't," replied Devlin, obviously worried.

"I'm sure Headmaster Lianon will have useful information for us. And there is probably a class to take or a book to read," said Lola, trying to lighten the mood.

"Or both!" said Devlin, getting up to stretch his long limbs. "Are there any bicycles here?" he asked.

"I'm not sure. If there were, they would be in the garage, I presume. Why?" asked Lola.

"I'm tired of sitting around. I need to move, or exercise," he said, swinging his arms back and front and walking around the patio.

"Do you want to go back to the pool and do some laps? I can lend you my goggles," suggested Lola.

"No, let's go check in the garage. I haven't seen it yet. And if we cross paths with Jackson, you won't be alone with him," he said with a wink.

"Fine, but we should change out of our bathing suits. And besides, I need my keys. Let's meet at the mudroom door in fifteen minutes," said Lola, and Devlin agreed.

They put their plates in the dishwasher and went upstairs to change.

Jackson was not on the Estate and the family car was not in the garage. Devlin was very impressed with the contents of the garage and took a moment to drool over the red Maserati. He gave a long whistle.

"I'm assuming you know this car?" asked Lola.

"Yes. It is a 1987 Maserati Biturbo Spyder and it is in perfect condition," he said reverently.

"Well, congratulations, it's yours! It was Dad's car and I won't be driving it anytime soon. Phyllis can't drive, so that leaves you. But wait until we have confirmation for the attorneys and insurance company," suggested Lola.

Devlin looked like a kid at Christmas. They moved away from the Maserati and combed the garage in search of bicycles. They came away empty-handed, but the visit was not in vain. Lola could tell Devlin would dream about the car that night.

"When we go back to the Townhouse, I'll bring the bicycles. Mother and I had recently upgraded ours and it would be a shame for them to just sit in the garage," he said. Lola shrugged. She wasn't sure about this bicycle business. She wasn't the most coordinated person and she hadn't been on a bike since she was eight years old.

It was almost two-thirty, so they headed back to the house. Marie had made cookies and they grabbed a couple while they waited for her to finish her shift. By the time they finished their snack, she was gone.

They raced into the foyer and separated their trunks so they would have more room to maneuver. Lola went first. She took out her key, thought of her room, and opened the door. She said a quick "Hello?" just in case. Of what, she had no idea. Devlin helped her push her trunk into her room and she closed the door.

"Now you. Make sure you picture your room in *this* house," she warned. Devlin gave her a sidelong glower and sighed. He took out his key and his door appeared. He opened the door, checked that it was the right room, pushed his trunk in, and closed the door.

"If I can get away with it, I may never use the stairs again!" said Lola as she opened her door again and walked in. She waved at Devlin and closed the door. Devlin was grinning like a Cheshire cat. He looked this way and that to ensure he was alone and did the same.

⁂

Back in her room, Lola put her dirty clothes in the hamper and put away the things she would be using at home. She left everything else in the trunk and pushed it back to its position at the foot of her bed.

Feeling thirsty, she cupped her hand and recited, *"Pugillo Aquas."* Her hand filled with water and she drank it. *This is fun!*

Then she decided to call Devlin with her mind. *Devlin, can you hear me?* She waited for a reply. After a while, she gave up and went to her alcove to get a pad of paper and a pen. She wanted to make a list of the most useful incantations so she could memorize them. *Look at me, giving myself homework on summer vacation. I'm such a nerd.*

She nearly fell down the winding stairs when she heard Devlin's telepathic reply, *Yes, you're a nerd, but it's a good idea. Can I join you?*

"Um, yeah," said Lola out loud. *Idiot,* she thought. *Excuse me?* he replied. *Not you, me. Come on over,* thought Lola.

Within minutes Devlin knocked and came into her room. She was waiting for him in the sitting room. He was carrying his books again.

"I think we should set aside some time to practice the incantations and to research telepathic abilities," suggested Devlin.

"Good idea. We can start with the Archives. I wonder where it is. We can also try the internet. Then check out the books here at the Mansion. And if we still need more, we can go into town to the public library. I'll introduce you to Bonnie, she's amazing," replied Lola.

They worked on their list for about an hour before calling it quits. They had to change for dinner and be down at six because they had a guest. Devlin asked if he needed to be fancier than the night before and Lola said no.

"I'll come to knock on your door at five-fifty-five so we can go down together, okay?" asked Devlin.

"Sure," replied Lola as she held the door open for him.

Lola brought her list to her alcove and put it in a drawer. With Marie cleaning and dusting, it was best not to leave things lying around. She took a few minutes to check her emails. Tom had sent a cute message saying he missed her and hoped she and Devlin had had a nice homecoming. Lola smiled and sighed. Checking her watch, she saw it was five-thirty here. That meant it was ten-thirty in Cork. He might read her reply before going to bed.

To: tom.callahan.gohurlers@gmail.com

From: lola4evers@gmail.com

Hi, Tom,

I miss you too! Things went well. Devlin and Phyllis took to one another immediately. Tonight we are having dinner with our attorney. We should get all the fine print out of the way. In fact, I should be changing for dinner as I write to you so I'll keep this short.

Sleep well,

Lola

She didn't have time to debate whether it was a lame message or not. She flew down the steps and into the bathroom to run a quick shower. She brushed her hair and braided it so it looked neater than her usual air-dry look. She grabbed a skirt and a blouse from her closet and threw them on, slipping her feet into ballerina flats. She checked herself in the mirror and was heading for the door when she heard the knock. She strode to the door and opened it. *Thank God it's you*, she thought.

Devlin smiled ruefully and extended his arm.

15

PAPERWORK

"It's a pleasure to meet you, sir," said Devlin as he shook hands with Edward Radcliff.

Devlin was nervous. As welcoming and generous as Lola and Phyllis had been, this was an attorney and he might not be so magnanimous. He wouldn't be doing his job if he didn't put in due diligence.

They sat in the parlor and Phyllis mixed a Tom Collins for Edward. Lola and Devlin both had ginger ales. Phyllis had an apple martini. They did a round of small talk and then the older gentleman reached for the briefcase that he had placed on the side of the armchair he was sitting in. He opened it and took out a leather portfolio. Returning his briefcase to the floor, he opened the portfolio and began, "I have quite a bit of information to impart tonight. Let's get straight to it." He took the first piece of paper and handed it to Phyllis.

"First, here is the shortlist of candidates for the housekeeper and groundskeeper positions. We've interviewed all the applicants and checked their references. These are the three couples we're recommending. All of them are available to start in August and are available for an interview this week," he said.

"But what about Jackson?" asked Lola.

"Jackson was accepted in the Business program at UVA last spring.

He had thought to delay his enrollment or enroll in part-time online classes so he could continue helping out here. As it stands, I thought it best to encourage him to enroll in the fall semester," said Phyllis. "He'll be staying on campus and coming home for long weekends and holidays," she added.

Devlin could see Lola was conflicted about this news, but she merely nodded. Then she raised her hand to interrupt again, "What about Marie? What will happen to her?" she asked.

"When Jackson's parents died, I was devastated and couldn't deal with hiring another couple, let alone see to having the cottage rebuilt. So we called an agency for a temporary replacement. That was three years ago.

"Marie's husband retired last year and has been after her to retire as well. She'll stay on to train the new housekeeper and then she'll get a well-deserved retirement package," said Phyllis soothingly, nodding at the attorney to continue.

"Next, I requested the blood samples that were taken at school and sent them to the lab. We were able to access Simon's records from when he was treated for cancer. They have confirmed paternity," he said and gave the sheet of paper he was holding to Devlin. "Congratulations, young man, you are now officially part of the Evers family," he said with a warm smile, and both Lola and Phyllis applauded.

"I want you to think about my next question carefully and you do not need to give me an answer immediately," stated the attorney. Devlin looked at Lola and she shrugged. Phyllis smiled knowingly and he was reassured.

"All right," he replied.

"Upon your birth, you were given your mother's surname. Today, I'd like to allow you to change it to Evers. It is your rightful name, but I understand you may want to keep the name you have lived with until now. You may keep your name, go by Johansson-Evers, or choose the Evers name," suggested Edward.

Everyone was silent as Devlin pondered this. He got up and paced around the room, his gaze resting on the portrait above the fireplace. Catching his gaze, Phyllis explained that Simon had painted it from a photograph. It depicted Simon and Phyllis, aged eight and ten, with their parents, standing in front of this very fireplace. He turned back to the attorney.

"Johansson was my mother's name and I shall wear it in my heart. Johansson-Evers is a bit of a mouthful and my parents were never really 'together' so it does not seem right to hyphenate their names. As they are both deceased, they are from the past. My old life ended on my eighteenth birthday. My new life should begin with a new name. I choose Evers," he concluded with a decided nod. Phyllis and Lola applauded again and he laughed.

"Very well. I had the papers drawn up in advance, planning for all three contingencies," said the attorney, waving three sets of identical stacks of paper. He chose the correct one, got up, and placed it on the coffee table with a pen. Devlin approached the table and signed or initialed each of the pages marked with a blue tab.

"I'll have these filed tomorrow. Once your legal name is changed, we'll apply for residency and identification," he said, putting the stack of papers back into his portfolio. He reached for his briefcase again and pulled out a large zippered pouch.

"In the meantime, here are the keys to the Mansion. Lola will explain," he said, giving Devlin a bunch of jangling keys.

"Here is your checkbook and an ATM bank card. A monthly allowance will be deposited there. I have been in contact with your attorney in Sweden. He has put your house up for sale and asks if you want to have your funds transferred to your American bank account," he asked.

"Yes, that would be more convenient, thank you," said Devlin, taking the checkbook and ATM card, a bit dazed.

"Here is a credit card for your use. It is a family card, meaning Lola and Phyllis have cards on the same account," Edward explained and handed the card over to Devlin. "Finally, as you are eighteen, the first portion of your inheritance has been deposited into your bank account. The next installment will come when you are twenty-one and the final one when you are thirty-five. Though that may change in the next few minutes," said the attorney cryptically.

Devlin frowned and asked, "What do you mean?" He really didn't care about the money, there was already so much of it he would never spend as it was.

"Our next piece of business concerns both Lola and Devlin," said the older gentleman, looking at each in turn. "Now that there is a male heir, and he is the older of the siblings, he is the rightful Custodian. I am told by the Headmaster that should Devlin not wish to be Custodian, he may transfer the responsibilities to Lola if she agrees. In addition to Custodian duties, which will be explained at the Academy, there are a few extra responsibilities here at the Mansion," said Edward. He pulled out a sheet of paper and gave it to Devlin so he could follow along. Devlin sat back down on the couch, next to Lola.

"First, the Evers Mansion must be your main residence until you have produced a male heir of age to replace you. Second, the Estate does not belong to you, it is entrusted to you for that duration. You must ensure the Estate prospers. That means seeing to its financial wellbeing as well as the upkeep of the property. Third, you are also ultimately responsible for all the Evers living in the Mansion. Though you *must* live here, other Evers may elect to live here or not. It is, however, their birthright to stay forever," explained the attorney, pausing to let that sink in. Devlin looked at Lola, who puffed out her cheeks and blew out in an expression that meant *Heavy, right?* Phyllis was wearing a serene expression on her face, as she had heard all this before.

Devlin turned back to Edward and asked, "When you say the main residence, what do you mean?"

"Evers Mansion must be your home. You may however temporarily live in one of your other homes. There's a list on the other side of that page. But never for more than six weeks at a time," said Edward.

"That seems reasonable," replied Devlin, and the attorney went on.

"Fourth, you must get married. At which point you would receive the second installment of your inheritance. A list of suitable candidates will be drawn up, but ultimately you are free to choose who you like. After my discussion with the Headmaster, it appears there might be other considerations to think about. Mainly about marrying another key holder, but we'll need to discuss this further at a later time. Fifth, you must have at least one child, though two or more would be better. Upon the birth of your firstborn, you would receive the third installment," concluded the attorney. He put the folder back into his briefcase.

"What if my wife and I are unable to have children?" asked Devlin, intent on the practicalities.

"Then you would not receive this installment, you would receive the same installment as your sibling. One of her children would become Custodian upon your death. If she had no children, then she would become Custodian. But that has never happened in the history of Evers thus far," explained Edward.

"May I have a moment to discuss this with Lola?" said Devlin, getting up and checking with Lola for confirmation.

"This issue doesn't need to be decided immediately," ventured Edward.

"I know. But we'll only take a moment," replied Devlin, grabbing Lola's hand and pulling her out into the hall and closing the door behind him.

"What do you want to do?" asked Devlin.

"It's ultimately your decision," hedged Lola.

"I see that. But I do not want to take something away from you that you truly want," he replied.

"Are you kidding! You'd be doing me a huge favor by taking on Custodianship. I was going out of my mind at the burden of it!" exclaimed Lola.

"Then it's settled," he said and turned towards the door but Lola put a hand on his arm to stop him.

"I'm sorry it's such a high price to pay," she said quietly.

"Not at all! I am honored to be given this opportunity to serve my family. I will do my duty with pride," he replied with a smile.

"Wow, you are much more honorable than I am!" said Lola.

"Do not take this the wrong way, but men usually are. We take on duty and responsibility more easily, it is in our genes. Just like caring and mothering is in yours," he stated.

Lola frowned. "We'll have to continue that discussion later. Right now, I'm starving," she said, reaching for the door handle.

"Of course you are," chuckled Devlin, reaching for the handle himself and opening the door for Lola and ushering her inside.

As they came back into the room, Phyllis looked surprised and said, "That was quick!"

"Indeed," replied Devlin. Then turning to the attorney he stood tall, shoulders back, and said, "It is an honor to accept Custodianship for this family and our heritage."

Edward nodded and looked at Phyllis, who smiled and announced, "Let's adjoin to the dining room."

16

TALK

Lola went back to her room after dinner to let it all settle. She and Devlin had agreed to have a movie night and a sleepover in the Nursery tonight, but she needed a few minutes to herself. Actually, what she needed was to talk to a girlfriend. But not Jane, because there was too much key-related business to discuss. No, this called for Sara. But it was near eight o'clock, which meant one in the morning in Gloucester. On impulse, Lola took out her phone and texted Sara.

Lola: Hey, can we have a face or phone chat tomorrow? That would be Tuesday. Tell me what time; I'm five hours behind you.

She put down her phone to grab her pajamas, but it buzzed immediately.

Sara: What's up?

Lola: Why are you still up?

Sara: I'm at a party...

Lola: Oh. Can you find a quiet spot for a five-minute chat?

Go ahead and ring me.

Lola hit the call button and Sara answered immediately. Lola realized belatedly that this might be an expensive call, but it was too late now. She would keep it short.

Lola: Hi Sara!

Sara: Hey Lola! It's good to hear your voice!

Lola: For me too. Look, I don't have a lot of time. Devlin is waiting for a movie night.

Sara: Go ahead. I'm listening.

Lola gave her a condensed version of everything that had happened since she got home. Jackson's welcome, the telepathy between her and Devlin, and the latest news about Custodianship.

Sara: So how do you feel about Jackson? I know you are probably ecstatic about relinquishing Custodian duties.

Lola: You're right! I mean, I was going to go back to the Academy in the fall so our plans wouldn't have worked anyway and I would never be home. I just feel bad for him. We haven't talked yet. I've been avoiding him. Maybe he thought we could have a long-distance relationship and see each other on holidays, like normal college kids.

Sara: Well, there's your problem! Stop overthinking this and go talk to the boy.

Lola: You're right.

Sara: Go now. I'll call Devlin to distract him while he waits for you to come back.

Lola: Good plan! Okay, let's talk again soon. I'll go before I change my mind. Thanks, Sara!

Sara: Anytime.

They hung up and Lola dashed across the hall to tell Devlin. Then as she headed down the stairs, she texted Jackson to ask if they could have a quick chat in the Gazebo. He responded immediately and said he would meet her there in five minutes.

When she passed the Library, she popped her head in to say good night to Phyllis. When Phyllis remarked she was going the wrong way, Lola explained about her meeting with Jackson. Phyllis made a soundless *Oh* and said, "Good luck!"

Lola went out by the patio door as it was closest to the Gazebo. She walked briskly, trying to think of what to say, only to realize that the best course of action was just to listen.

She and Jackson arrived at the same time. There was an awkward moment where they didn't seem to know how to greet one another. But

Lola decided a quick hug would be fine and set the tone. She stepped forward and said, "Hi", her arms extended slightly. Jackson got the idea and wrapped her in a bear hug. It only lasted a moment and already Lola felt herself want to merge with him, to cling to his body heat. It was unnerving. She disengaged and took a step back, heading for one of the benches. There were twinkle lights suspended in the eaves of the Gazebo and the lighting was just enough to see each other, without being too stark.

"I guess you found out about UVA," he said and Lola nodded.

"I guess you found out about the new caretakers," she said and Jackson nodded.

"It's better this way. We'll both be going away to school in the fall and coming home only a few times per year," explained Jackson and Lola said nothing, hoping he would continue.

"It's a four-year program and I think you've got at least that many years ahead of you. We're both still very young and now that there is no pressing need to get married, I think we should each find our own path. If that path leads us back to each other, then it won't have been in vain. If it doesn't, then that will mean it wasn't meant to be," he said. "What do you think?" he asked.

"I think you are much more mature than I am. You're right, of course. It was insane to fall in love and talk about marriage after less than a week. This sounds much more reasonable. And it will let us focus on our studies instead of pining away for each other. Besides, you still live here, right? And there's still a whole month of summer left!" said Lola, warming up to this new plan.

"About that. Yes, I still live here and Phyllis said it will be my home for as long as I want it. She asked that I show Devlin what I've been doing in terms of investments and the new security. I'll do that next week. After that, I'll be taking a vacation for a few weeks before school starts. It was Phyllis' suggestion."

"Oh. Where are you going?"

"I'm going to visit Italy, Switzerland, and Austria. I really enjoyed it when we went to Florence and wanted to go back. I'll be staying in the family's apartments while I'm there, so I'll only need to pay for food and expenses. Phyllis gave me the plane ticket as a birthday present," he said.

"Wow, so it's all settled," said Lola. She didn't know if she was sad or relieved. And she didn't want to have to figure it out just then. She got up quickly and thanked him for meeting with her.

"Devlin is waiting for me for movie night. Do you want to join us?" she offered.

"No, you spend some quality time with your brother. Maybe some other time," he said and gave her a quick kiss on the temple.

"Good night, Lola," he said with a sad smile.

"Good night, Jackson," she replied, a similar expression on her face and headed back to the house.

The whole conversation had taken less than fifteen minutes. She slipped into the kitchen and locked the door. When she passed the Library, it was empty. She made her way upstairs and found Devlin, pajama-clad, chatting on the phone with Sara. She raised her hand, meaning five minutes, and Devlin nodded. That would be enough time for her to get her pajamas on while he ended the call.

"Sara filled me in. How was your chat with Jackson?" asked Devlin.

"It went well. He did most of the talking," she replied.

"What did he say?" asked Devlin.

"That we are too young to commit, should go to college and live our lives. If our paths cross later, then it's meant to be. That's the super short version. I know you don't like it when I go on and on," joked Lola.

"Thank you, I appreciate it," he said with a smile. "Are you all talked out?" he asked.

"Yes! Is it too late for a movie?" she asked. He shook his head and pointed to the screen.

"I have a few suggestions here on the streaming service," he said.

"Let's have a look," she replied, grabbing the remote from his hands.

She flipped through the top ten choices while Devlin pointed out the ones he was interested in. They were both pleased to note that they had two movie genres in common: Fantasy /Sci-Fi and Action/Adventure. It made choosing a movie easier. And since they'd both been so busy with school and parental drama, they hadn't seen any of the latest movies.

Lola asked if he wanted any popcorn or soda. Devlin didn't want to go back down to the kitchen and it was getting late.

"Ah, but I have found a secret stash!" she said and motioned for him to follow her into the Schoolroom. In one of the wall-to-ceiling storage doors, there was a mini-fridge. She had stashed a few bottles of water and cola here when Jane was here, and there were still plenty. On top of the fridge were some mini chip bags, individually wrapped bags of candy, and microwaveable popcorn packs.

"This is like having our very own cinema!" cried Devlin. He grabbed a popcorn pack and started reading the instructions. Lola took it out of his hands, removed the plastic wrapper, placed it face up in the microwave, and pressed the 'Popcorn' setting.

"Sorry, it's faster this way. What kind of candy do you like?" she asked.

"All of them! Some of these are new to me, and I had very little to begin with. My mother had us on a very healthy diet," he said, grabbing a bag of chips and a couple of candy bags. Lola got the same but chose different kinds so they could share. They both took bottled water and went back to the sofa to set their loot down. Devlin went back for the popcorn while Lola set up the movie they had decided on: a fantasy film about time travel.

They settled in and made it to the end of the movie without falling asleep. Lola was happy because she really wanted to brush her teeth after ingesting so much sugar.

"Still want to sleep in here?" she asked.

"Yes, of course. I've never slept in bunkbeds!" he exclaimed, giddy with excitement.

"Really? That's incredible! Let me just brush my teeth and wash my face. Back in a flash," she said and ran out of the room. He leaped to his feet and called out, "I will race you," and then ran past her down the hall.

"You're on!" she replied, darting into her room.

17

PIZZA

The next morning, Lola had a plan. She woke up and did her meditation and her yoga in her room. At five past eight, she crept down the stairs in her pajamas. Devlin and Phyllis were out in the Gazebo, Marie was in the kitchen, and there was no one in the Sunroom. *Yes!*

She sneaked in and got a cup of coffee. Later she would ask Marie for a thermos, there would be more coffee! She also grabbed a banana and a muffin impulsively, which she wrapped in a napkin. *Apple cinnamon, yum.* Feeling like a thief, she checked the hall. The coast was clear, and she walked briskly to the stairs and made a beeline for her room. *Success!*

She spent the next two hours reading in bed and trying not to get any crumbs between the sheets.

She washed up, dressed, and went down to have breakfast with her family at ten, smiling and serene. Neither Phyllis nor Devlin commented on her absence nor her good mood. They knew what was good for them.

"For the next few days, after breakfast, I will be meeting Jackson in the Library. He will explain the tasks he has been doing so that I can take over," announced Devlin, barely suppressing his pride.

"That's wonderful, sugar," said Phyllis.

"And in the afternoons, I will sort the things I want to keep from the townhouse. The rest will be sold or given away," he explained.

"Do you need help? Should I come with you?" asked Lola.

"Not today. I will do my room first. But perhaps tomorrow you will help me with my mother's room . . ." he trailed, a sad look on his face.

"I can come too," said Phyllis. "I remember how hard it was to deal with Simon's things after he died. As you saw, I didn't do a very good job of it; I kept almost everything!" she said, trying for humor. "But eventually, it will need to be sorted. Whoever takes over as Custodian will likely want to move into that room since the other rooms are meant for their children."

"I will accept your help tomorrow then," said Devlin. "And when the time comes, we will deal with Father's room together," he added with an encouraging smile.

For the next couple of days, that was their routine. Lola spent a little time every morning helping Phyllis in the garden. It gave them time to chat, just the two of them. Later, Lola would head for the pool to do some laps and work on her tan. Now that Lola and Jackson were back in the friend zone, it was easier to be around him. The four of them would have lunch together after the 'Estate' lessons, as Devlin called them. Though Devlin and Jackson had gotten off to a rocky start, once Devlin's claim had been substantiated by the attorney, Jackson hadn't been quite so hostile to him. In the evenings, however, Jackson did not join them for dinner.

Devlin's attorney had sent someone to the Townhouse on Monday. When he arrived on Tuesday, things were already easier to deal with. They had left packing boxes and tape, as well as tall wardrobe boxes. Devlin quickly packed up his room and anything he wanted to keep from around the Townhouse. When he was done, all he had to do was open a door to his room at the Mansion. He put a doorstop so the door would remain open. He didn't know how long a door could remain open, so he repeated the exercise every five minutes or so until he'd moved everything. It wasn't that much.

When Phyllis and Lola came the next day, he asked Phyllis to sort through his mother's clothes. She should put anything worth giving to charity in a wardrobe box and the rest she should just throw out. His mother's clothing was of good quality, but old and not very fashionable. While Phyllis set out on this task, Devlin and Lola went to the garage to move the bicycles.

"I think we should open a door near the fountain in front of the Mansion," suggested Lola. "I don't want to take any chances of opening a door right in the garage. This way, we can simply ride the bikes to the garage," she added. Devlin agreed.

They opened a door and Lola crossed over and held the door open while Devlin pushed the bike through, letting go once Lola had it and holding the door so she could set it on its stand. They did the same with the second bike and stored them in the garage. Jackson wasn't around.

Back at the Townhouse, they joined Phyllis again. She had completed the task and had started packing books and other non-personal items in a box.

They spent the next couple of hours cleaning out the rest of the house.

When they were done, Devlin went back to the garage to put the trash in the bins and roll them to the curb.

Other than the car, the garage was mostly empty. There was nothing personal in the utility room either.

When he got back upstairs, Lola was done with the cabinets, and Phyllis was done with his mother's room. They stacked the boxes along the main wall of the living room and declared they were done.

"This calls for pizza!" exclaimed Lola.

"Oh yes! I know just the place!" replied Phyllis, rubbing her hands together in anticipation.

"Lead the way!" replied Devlin, taking one last look at his old life and thanking his lucky stars.

Phyllis opened a door and they followed her through. However, once on the other side, they were outside the Evers Mansion. Phyllis opened the door again and motioned for them to follow. It was dark where they were going. Gingerly, Lola went through the door and moved to the side to let Devlin come through.

"Where are we?" asked Lola, though the cobblestone street was looking familiar. "Are we in Florence?" she squeaked.

"Well, we are in Italy, that is certain," said Devlin looking around him.

"Yes, we're in Italy. No, it's not Florence, silly, it's Naples!" she exclaimed, throwing her arms wide and spinning.

"But it must be close to eleven, are the restaurants still open?" asked Lola.

Both Devlin and Phyllis laughed at this. "What's so funny?" she asked, narrowing her eyes. She was miffed at being laughed at.

"Most restaurants do not open for dinner before eight or nine. Yes, they are still open and will surely be full!" replied Devlin.

Lola looked around and was unimpressed with her surroundings. They were in some kind of walled area that was a cross between an alley and a parking lot. She saw a gate with a sign.

"Does that say Psychiatric Diagnosis and Cure?" she exclaimed in disbelief.

"Well done, darling. That's exactly what it says. Isn't it the perfect place to arrive? Who's going to believe anyone saying they saw us coming out of a door that appeared out of nowhere!" said Phyllis, nearly cackling. Lola's eyes grew wide and she inched closer to Devlin. He thought it was hilarious.

"Come along, children. It's only a block away," said Phyllis, briskly walking toward the street.

They followed her closely, and Lola was relieved that the decor improved immediately once they reached the side street, and even more so once they got to the Piazza Sanità.

"This is lovely," whispered Lola as they arrived in front of the restaurant. There was a beautiful outdoor seating area under an awning with growing vines and potted plants.

"Here it is; the Pizzeria Oliva da Salvatore e Carla, the best pizza in

Naples," exclaimed Phyllis. "Eat here or to go?" she asked, looking to Devlin, then to Lola.

"Here!" they both said in unison.

They had to wait a bit to be seated, so they read the menu while they waited. When they were seated and the waiter had taken their drink orders, they had already decided what they wanted, so Phyllis ordered for all of them. Devlin chose a *Pazzarella*, which was topped with courgettes, meatballs, and provolone cheese. Lola chose a *Ripieno Fritto*, a pizza topped with mozzarella, ricotta, provolone cheeses, with salami and fresh tomatoes. Phyllis ordered a pizza *Al Prosciutto Crudo*: tomato, mozzarella, and parma ham.

When the wine arrived, the waiter served each of them a glass without batting an eye.

After he had gone, Lola whispered, "Shouldn't he be checking if we are of legal drinking age?"

Devlin replied, "In most European countries, the legal drinking age is sixteen, and it is never checked or enforced, as it is much more important to be with family and friends, having a good meal and a good time." He took his glass and raised it. "Saluti," he said loudly. Phyllis did the same and clinked her glass with his and they both looked at Lola expectantly. Lola sighed and said, "When in Rome!" Then she raised her glass and repeated, "Saluti!"

The pizza was amazing and they had a really good time. Phyllis paid with her credit card and they walked slowly back towards the back alley. On the way, Lola saw a gelato stand and made puppy eyes at Phyllis, who could only laugh at her niece's antics.

"How are you even still hungry?" she asked in amazement.

"Don't you know the dessert box rule?" asked Lola, pulling them both toward the gelato stand.

"It's like a sidecar to your stomach, but only for desserts. When you reach adulthood, it usually turns into common sense," she explained, deadpan.

Phyllis hooted with laughter and took Lola in her arms. "You are adorable, darling," she said, kissing Lola on the temple. "Go ahead and have your gelato. In fact, let's all have some gelato!" she exclaimed.

"*Un gelato al limone per favore*," said Lola proudly to the girl at the window. Then she turned to the others and said, "I can order yours too!" Phyllis requested a hazelnut-flavored ice cream and Devlin asked for one with a tiramisu flavor.

They walked around and ate their gelato in contented bliss. Once they were done, they went to the alley and Traveled home.

18

ARCHIVES

The next morning at breakfast Phyllis put a pocket watch on the table.

"I found this when I went to water the plants in Simon's room," she said.

Lola and Devlin peered at the pocket watch. It was clearly an antique, smaller than a typical pocket watch, the size of a large pendant. The back of the gold case was intricately carved with a central E looped into an infinity sign.

"*Evers are Forever*, the family motto," said Lola, reverently.

Devlin flipped it over to reveal the front of the timepiece. The carvings on this side depicted an hourglass with a small key resting on the sand at the bottom of the hourglass.

"Is this what I think it is?" asked Lola, grabbing the watch and opening it. It was double-sided. Both sides were identical, but the carvings on one of the inside covers read *Ancestors* while the other read *Descendants*. She gave the watch to Devlin so he could look at it more closely. He was nodding. *Yes, I think it is*, he replied to Lola.

"This must be how Dad Traveled through time. Where did you find it?" asked Lola, turning to Phyllis.

"That's the odd thing—on the floor next to his bedside table. Marie cleans in there every week and I water the plants a few times per week, and it never showed up before," she replied, perplexed.

"When we did the tour, I gave Devlin the family Bible to look at. Maybe it fell out of the drawer and we didn't notice," suggested Lola.

"Either way, we were meant to find it. And since I have his wrist-watch, Lola should have the pocket watch. It is clearly meant to be worn around the neck and she is the Time Walker . . ." said Devlin, standing to put it around Lola's neck. The gold chain was long enough that it didn't need to be unfastened. It settled right on her breast bone.

"Besides, now you will not need to keep asking what time it is," he said with a laugh.

"Does it tell time do you think?" asked Lola, seriously. She peered into the inner workings of the Ancestors' side, which would be seen through the glass. Each side had a main knob, like a regular pocket watch, to adjust the time and wind it. But upon closer inspection, she saw there were tiny gold arms that could be rotated left or right. There were also three rows of letters, numbers, and symbols that she had initially taken for decorative carvings.

"We will need a magnifying glass to study this properly," said Lola. Then her face illuminated as she thought of an idea. She removed the watch from around her neck and placed it on the table. She removed her phone from her pocket and tapped the photo app. She took multiple close-range pictures of all angles of the timepiece.

"We can zoom in on the phone and also blow them up on a computer and even print the pictures to study it," she said proudly.

"When can I see the Archives?" asked Devlin.

No sooner had he said it, than the massive book landed with a plop in front of him, barely missing his discarded breakfast plate. He stared at it, dumbfounded.

"It never did that for me!" exclaimed Lola.

"You were never the Custodian," replied Phyllis, laughing lightly.

"It came like this when Simon called it?" asked Devlin, incredulously.

"Well, no. The book was usually kept in the vault at the attorneys' office. When Simon was sick, he requested the book be brought to him.

I don't think it ever occurred to him to call it," said Phyllis, looking astonished.

"That is so cool!" said Lola. "Open it!" she urged.

Devlin put a finger delicately under the bottom corner of the cover and lifted. It wouldn't budge. He grabbed the book with both hands and tried to part the pages somewhere in the middle; still no luck.

"Perhaps you should introduce yourself. Speak your full name," suggested Phyllis.

They watched in rapt attention as Devlin squared his shoulders and said, "Joseph Devlin Johansson Evers."

There was a shimmer in the air above the book and it shook slightly. The cover opened to the second page and Devlin saw his name recorded under his father's name. He smiled and turned the book to show Lola and Phyllis, beaming.

The page turned itself and Devlin stared at the blank page. When words started to appear, Devlin read them out loud in case they disappeared again before Lola and Phyllis could read them.

"Dearest Devlin,

The Ancestors welcome their newest Custodian. You are the keeper of the Keys and of this book we call the Archives. It is both an instruction manual and a chronicle of Custodians' passed. The content is ever expanding and will adapt to your specific needs. Hence, since you are a World Jumper and your sibling is a Time Walker, these topics have been added. Furthermore, as you possess telepathic abilities, you may produce verbal requests for the book and it will open to the appropriate page or section. Your sibling and guardian may consult the book only in your presence. Should there be another present, the book will either remain closed or appear blank to the intruder. While every care has--"

They heard footsteps in the hall and the book closed itself. Before it disappeared to unknown parts again, Devlin told it to go to his room. It vanished and he hoped it had gone to the correct place.

Jackson popped his head into the Sunroom. "Phyllis, Edward is on the phone for you," he said. Phyllis got up, excused herself, and told Lola and Devlin they could resume their discussion after lunch.

Devlin checked the time and looked at Jackson. "It is time for the

Estate lessons, correct?" he asked. Jackson laughed and nodded. "Come on buddy, we're almost done," he said. Then to Lola, he said, "Good morning, Lola." She responded in kind and got up.

When Jackson and Devlin headed for the Library, Lola headed to the kitchen to ask Marie where she could find a thermos.

"What do you need a thermos for?" the elderly housekeeper asked.

Lola explained her idea, and Marie had an even better solution.

"Why don't I make you a pot of coffee. We've got one of those carafes that keeps the coffee warm and can hold about four cups," she suggested.

"That would be divine!" squealed Lola.

"I'll leave the tray on the kitchen counter with cream, sugar, and a little snack to hold you over," she said with a wink.

"Thank you, Marie! You're the best," said Lola as she skipped out of the kitchen.

Devlin and Jackson were in the Library pouring over Jackson's laptop. They had gone over the physical files in the Library, and those stored in the attic. Jackson had made a list of the daily, weekly, monthly, and annual tasks he performed and had explained each in detail. Everything was in a neat binder on the desk in the Library. What they were looking at now, was the investment software Jackson used to keep track, buy, and sell their stocks. Devlin looked uneasy. No one had mentioned day trading. Jackson said they had financial advisors for the larger envelopes. Jackson had requested permission to manage a smaller portion of the assets to invest in sustainable markets.

"But you don't actually have to manage any of the assets. You only have to meet with the brokerage firm once every quarter to review their progress and make any changes in the orientation you might want," he said. At Devlin's confused expression, he added," Like investing more in education, or agriculture, for example." Devlin nodded.

"But don't worry, Phyllis also attends the meetings and she will likely continue to attend them until you are at least twenty-one, or until such time as you are both confident that you can manage on your own," he advised.

"And that's pretty much it," he concluded. "Tomorrow I'll let you handle the dailies and some of the weeklies and I'll stick around to answer any questions. We'll do that next week too until you get the hang of it. How does that sound?" he asked.

"It sounds like a good plan. Thank you for your patient instruction, Jackson," replied Devlin.

"No problem, buddy," he said. "I'm starving, let's go see about lunch," he suggested.

19

EVERS

After breakfast, Lola took the watch to her room and snapped many, many pictures with both her phone and her iPad. She printed out the sharpest images.

She spent the morning poring over the images and making notes in one of her leather-bound journals. She spent hours researching online for similar watches or any mention of time travel, but only found fiction.

What was bothering her was that Simon had lied. He had said he wasn't quite sure how he was able to visit her in the future. He never mentioned the watch. Did he mean that he had accidentally got the watch to work but didn't know how to change any of the settings?

Lola was dying to look at the Archives. Surely if Simon was a Time Walker, he would have found the chapters on Time Travel in the book. It was bound to explain how to use the watch. Then again, neither Phyllis nor Simon had known anything about the Academy. Also, it was Edward who had suggested that Simon look for incantations in the book. Edward had been more familiar with the Archives than Simon had. Simon might have barely looked at the book until he got sick and had to stay near to home.

Phyllis, Lola, and Devlin met in the Schoolroom after lunch to continue the morning's exploration of the book. Once they were seated, Devlin called the book and it appeared.

Lola and Phyllis applauded and Devlin puffed out his chest a little. He turned to the page where he had started reading the welcoming message. Devlin was relieved to see it was still there and continued to read out loud for the ladies.

"While every care has been taken to provide a comprehensive and accurate guide for new Custodians, should you not find a satisfactory answer to an inquiry, you may call upon the Council of Elders. Since there are numerous Custodians around the world, they have been divided into smaller Councils of ten to twelve Custodians. You need not be elderly to be an Elder. The term means Head of the Family.

Many generations ago, Custodians would start training their sons upon their eighteenth birthday and retire as soon as the youth was ready to take over the duties. The former Custodians would then join the Council of Elders.

Between wars, famine, pestilence, and witch hunts, Elders were dying before they could pass on the knowledge, or their heirs died before they could receive it or even produce children of their own. Family lines were broken and the Keys disappeared.

One day, the remaining Elders met with the Council of Earthly Magical Beings to request their assistance. A solution was proposed: To create an educational establishment in a safe location where Travelers could learn about their heritage and Custodians about their responsibilities. There would also be instruction for the rarer Time Walkers and World Jumpers.

Most of the Elders agreed with the plan and they began pooling their knowledge to produce a book which they called the Archivum. Since their lifespans were much longer than those of humans, the Archivum was entrusted to the Council of Earthly Magical Beings who agreed to host the school, update the Archivum, and train the children.

However, one of the Elders, Archibald, did not agree with this plan, though he did not initially make his objections known. He waited until the Archivum was completed; it took many months. The Elders would meet three times per week and took turns writing out the information that should be added to the book. A scribe was hired to produce the final copy so that it was legible and uniform. For a month, the scribe lived in the Elders' meeting house so that he may complete his task, unobserved and undisturbed.

Since Archibald was a very affluent man, he paid the scribe to translate the notes from Latin to English. Sworn to secrecy, the scribe wrote a second copy, in English, of the requested manuscript. When the task was completed, the Elder paid the scribe and disappeared with the leather-bound volume.

He sailed to the Colonies and settled in Jamestown. Since his wife and child had died of the Plague in England, he set out alone on this adventure. While many of his countrymen struggled in the colony, he was thriving, due mostly to his ability to Travel and get provisions from all over the world instead of having to rely on trade ships.

In 1697, he met Emmeline Evers, a witch who had escaped the witch trials unharmed. Partly because she was a powerful witch who could elude notice, partly because she was the daughter of Lord John Evers, a prominent landowner. Lady Emmeline was much younger than Archibald and quite beautiful. She had a good many suitors. But she could sense the magic about him and was inclined to accept his proposal, thinking he would be more open-minded and she would not need to control him with magic.

To test his character, on one of their outings, she told him she was an only child and would inherit her father's Estate. Should they marry, he would have control of her fortune. She asked him if he would consider giving their children the Evers name so that her legacy could live on for future generations. He not only agreed but said that when her father died, he would change his own name to Evers. They were married the following spring.

In 1699, Lord Evers died. Archibald and his now-pregnant wife moved into the Evers Mansion in Williamsburg, then the Capital of Virginia. As promised, Archibald set out to change his name to Evers.

The Estate had an attorney on retainer, a young man named George Radcliff. The paperwork was filed and Archibald became Archibald Evers, the first of the Ancestors."

Devlin stopped reading. He had taken a few short breaks while reading to drink from the water bottle Lola had set before him. Both Phyllis and Lola had been in rapt attention and blinked when they realized he had stopped reading.

"Is that all? What happened next? What about the Keys, the watch, and the marble? No mention of them?" she asked, trying to peer closer at the book from where she sat.

"Darling, there must be over a thousand pages in that book. I'm sure there are answers to your questions in there somewhere," said Phyllis patiently.

"Well, it explains the mystery behind the book being in English and why no Evers has attended the Academy. We are rebels!" he exclaimed.

"And, it would seem, part witch," said Lola.

"Perhaps that's where you get the telepathy abilities," suggested Phyllis. "This is all very exciting. To think we've been Traveling for years without knowing any of this!" she added.

"While Devlin catches his breath, how about I show you the pictures I took of the watch," proposed Lola. She took them out of the folder and spread them out on the table.

"Once blown up, the images reveal a lot," she started. "Look, this one is from the Ancestors' side. There are actually six rows of symbols and numbers. The first runs from one to thirty-one, so it's obviously the day. The second is months, see the letters here?" said Lola, pointing on the picture to the letters J through D. "The next four are numerals from 0 to 9, which I believe are for the year. When I touched the watch, I could feel each of the dials. The question is if you want to Travel to a specific hour in a day, do you just think about it as you think of the location? Or do you go at the same time as the current time?" asked Lola, to no one in particular.

But the book was listening and it opened to a page about Traveling to the past. Lola shot up and made a grab for the book. It didn't recoil or disappear. She held it more loosely and read the passage.

"The Time Walker arrives at the same time as the local time from whence he came. One should, therefore, make the necessary calculations in advance to avoid arriving at an inopportune time.

The Time Walker will return within one minute of his departure time, regardless of how much time one has spent in the past. There are no rules as to the length of time one can spend in the past. It is preferable that one not stay past their date of birth. There is no corporeal danger. However, should one's presence in the time leading to one's birth have somehow created a ripple, it may have an impact on the events of one's childhood or life experiences which would, in turn, change who one becomes in the future. Since the future Time Walker is currently living in the past, one would become confused beyond measure and may, in fact, go mad."

"Ok, so no Traveling during your own lifetime, got it," said Lola, bracing her hands on the table.

"What about the future? Do you have to wait until your future self is dead to visit it?" asked Devlin.

The book flipped ahead a few pages and waited for them to read the answer.

"When Traveling to the future, there is no need to avoid one's lifespan. One may, if one so desires, visit with oneself, taking care to visit after one has been made aware that one is a Time Walker to avoid any unnecessary distress. Since the future is yet to be produced, there is no danger in interacting with oneself. Unless one has already visited a much farther future. Then we would recommend that one not get too attached to that future, as it will likely change. Therein lies the conundrum of Traveling to the future--it is as fleeting as the sand escaping an hourglass."

"An attempt at humor? Or perhaps philosophy?" quipped Devlin.

Phyllis got up from the chair and started to stretch her arms up over her head.

"Most likely the musings of an experienced Time Walker who has been disappointed time and again by his sojourns into the future," she said. "I don't know about you two, but I've had more than enough of sitting and I believe I've reached my saturation point with this business," she concluded. Checking her watch, she added, "I'm going for a walk by the River Thames, there is about a half-hour before sunset and the colors are magnificent. I'll see you at dinner!" She blew a kiss in their general direction and left the room.

"Phyllis is right, we've been cooped up inside all day. We should get some fresh air," suggested Lola.

"Where would you like to go? We can go for a walk, go swimming in the pool, or ride the bicycles to visit the town. You could introduce me to Bonnie at the Library. Or, we could Travel somewhere," said Devlin, a mischievous look in his eye.

"Those are all good options. Did you have a specific Travel destination in mind?" she asked, trying to read his thoughts—but he wasn't sharing.

"There are so many places I want to visit, but I do not think we have enough practice to go to places we have not been to before. Also, I would love to take you to see my favorite places in Stockholm, but we would need at least a day for that," he replied.

"To the Library on our bicycles, then. You realize I may need a refresher course and some training wheels," she said, getting up and gathering the photos from the table.

Devlin closed the book and tucked it under his arm.

"It will come back to you, I am certain. Shall we meet in front of the garage in fifteen minutes?" he asked. Lola nodded and they went to their rooms to change.

20

BIKES

The old cliché was right, riding a bike DID come back to her, and, after checking the directions on their phones, the pair was off. It was fairly straightforward and it took them about thirty minutes because they were able to cut through a large field and use the bike path which conveniently led right to the Library.

"We can only spend about an hour and a half in town if we want to get home in time to shower and change for dinner," said Lola. "Maybe I should give you a quick tour of the town before we go into the Library. It's sometimes hard to leave once I go in there," she added with a laugh.

He agreed and they locked their bikes on the rack in front of the Library. She showed him the grocery store where she worked for a couple of days, some of Phyllis' favorite shops, and the town Gazebo. It was a short tour. They made their way back to the Library and went in.

Bonnie was wearing her usual roller skates and when Lola introduced Devlin as her brother, she nearly fell right there on the spot. Devlin grabbed her arm to steady her and asked if she was all right.

"Well, color me flabbergasted! Where did you say you were from, sugar?" she said, righting herself and staring up at Devlin's angelic face.

"I am from Sweden. It is a long story," he said with a laugh.

"Come on and tell me while I give you the tour," she said, waving them along.

It was the same tour she had given Lola, only this time she lingered and gave more details on some of the local history since Jackson wasn't there rolling his eyes and checking his watch. When they got to the little locked room, Devlin asked her if he could pop in for a quick look. Bonnie laughed and said, "He really is your brother!"

"So y'all met at summer camp like in The Parent Trap?" Bonnie joked.

"I guess you could say that, though we're not twins. Devlin is eighteen."

She led them back to the counter and asked if he wanted a library card.

"Yes, please!" said Devlin, overjoyed.

Bonnie typed into the computer, scanned the card, and held it out to him.

"Don't lose it, sugar, or it'll cost you five dollars to replace it. This one's on the house!" she said with a wink. Devlin took the card and thanked her.

"There's a bonfire out at Patty's farm tonight if you wanna come," she said, more to Devlin than to Lola.

"First, who is Patty? Where is his farm? And what time is the bonfire at?" asked Lola, not entirely sure how to respond.

"Patty is Patricia Wilcox. She went to school with Jackson and me. You haven't met her yet because she was traveling to Europe with her boyfriend's family when the summer season began. And her daddy's farm is about five miles out of town, heading East. I can text you the address. Bonfire starts at sundown, so I'd guess around nine pm. It's BYOC," she said.

Devlin looked at Lola, but she didn't know either.

"What's BYOC?" she asked.

"Bring Your Own Chair, silly," she replied.

"Right! Text me the details. I'll check with Phyllis to see what's up tonight and let you know," replied Lola casually, knowing full well there was only a very slim chance they would attend the bonfire. She'd need to confer with Devlin, but she was pretty sure it was a pass for him too.

They said their goodbyes and left the Library. Once they were riding their bikes, Lola asked Devlin what he thought of the bonfire idea.

"I'm not sure. I like Bonnie very much, but I have a feeling the crowd at the bonfire will be the kind that drinks too much and talks too loud. Besides, we are often exhausted by nine o'clock and get up early in the morning," he said.

"Yeah, I totally agree. I guess we're the lamest teenagers in the county!" exclaimed Lola. "Besides, we have no idea what we're in for at the house party this Saturday," she added.

"That's true. I had forgotten. And we are entertaining guests tomorrow night, correct?" he asked. Lola nodded and quickly texted Bonnie that they would not be able to make it.

"Yes, the kids are Sheila and Matthew. They're super nice. Dinner takes a long time, but last time we went out on the porch after and played card games."

"In Sweden, my friends and I would meet to play games and, aside from tournaments, our evenings never ended very late," put in Devlin.

"What kind of games?" asked Lola

"Video games like Minecraft and Diavolo, but also games like Dungeons and Dragons, Stratego, and chess. Do you play chess, Lola?" said Devlin.

"Wow, no wonder you got along with James and Colin! I'm really bad at chess, but if you want to play, you can ask Jackson before he leaves. Or you could try to teach me," she said with a laugh.

"Yes, I would love to teach you. Is there a set at home?" he asked.

"In the Library," replied Lola.

They biked in silence for a while before Lola broke the silence.

"Aren't you curious about how to World Jump with your marble?" she asked.

"Perhaps not as much as you are about Time Walking because the

Headmaster explained it to me and showed me how it works on his portal," he replied. "But I am anxious to try it!" he admitted.

"But do you think you need a portal?" she asked.

"We can ask the book later if you want," he said with a chuckle.

"This was a good idea. Left to my own devices I would probably still be hunched over that book, scribbling notes like a mad scientist," said Lola, taking a deep inhale of fresh country air and exhaling contentedly.

"Yes, it is quite pretty here. The flora is different from back in Sweden," replied Devlin.

"How so?" asked Lola.

"Well, being in the south, it's very lush and luxuriant here with ferns, shrubs, and vines. Most of Sweden is covered by coniferous trees, mainly spruce and pine. The southern part of the country has some deciduous trees, such as beech, oak, elm, ash, and maple. The climate resembles that of New England," he said, taking in his surroundings.

"I don't know about plants and vegetation, but that sounds about right. I lived in Baltimore before moving here and vegetation was sparse," she replied with a laugh. "Phyllis is really into gardening. There are probably lots of books on the topic in the Library if you are interested," she suggested.

"Mother had a green thumb. She was part of the community garden," he said, remembering fondly. "But I was never that interested, other than eating the vegetables she brought home, that is," he said enthusiastically.

"I'm with you there. Everything that comes out of Phyllis' garden is delicious. Much more so than any vegetables I've ever had from the store. It's great that she can grow it year round," said Lola.

They turned into the lane that led to the Mansion and returned the bikes to the garage. Going in through the mudroom, they walked past the kitchen. It smelled really good. Like garlic or onions, but everything was spotless. Dinner must be in the oven.

They headed up to shower and change.

"After dinner, I'd like to go through your wardrobe with you Devlin, sugar, to see what we may need to purchase for the rest of the season," said Phyllis as they sat down to dinner. On the menu that night was a dish of spinach and ricotta cannelloni, garlic bread, and a green salad. To Lola's utter delight, they were having peach cobbler à la mode for dessert. It was Devlin's first taste and he was hooked.

"This is delicious, Phyllis. Did you cook all of this yourself?" asked Devlin.

"I'm afraid not, sugar. This is all Marie's doing," replied Phyllis. "All I did was toss the salad and put the Lasagna in the oven to warm it, and then the cobbler. I'll be sure to tell Marie you enjoyed it," she added.

"I'll tell her myself tomorrow!" he replied.

"Phyllis is an excellent cook. She made our dinner on Sunday night. She makes most of our weekend meals. But it looks like she'll get a break Saturday night and Sunday morning," said Lola with a wink.

"Which reminds me," said Phyllis. "I'll be interviewing the three couples tomorrow morning. Devlin, I know you'll be busy with Jackson. But Lola, would you mind sitting in on the interviews?"

"Sure, I'd love to," replied Lola.

"That is fine with me. I would not know which questions to ask. And if I think of something, I'll tell Lola," he said with a wink.

"Good, it's best if I'm not making this decision alone," said Phyllis.

They discussed the afternoon's revelations from the book and wondered when they would resume reading it.

"I think it'll have to wait until Monday," said Lola, obviously chagrined. "Tomorrow morning we have the interviews, then shopping, then dinner with the Maxwells. Saturday morning we'll need to pack and get ready for the house party, and we'll be back at lunchtime Sunday. I'm assuming we'll be tired. Sunday night, Jackson will be dining with us, so we won't be able to discuss anything in great detail," concluded Lola.

"If you two want to keep exploring without me, you go ahead. Just keep me updated on your findings," said Phyllis.

"I believe Lola is right. It will have to wait until Monday. I prefer that you be included in the initial exploration. Later, Lola and I can ask the book for clarifications and details," said Devlin, looking to Lola for confirmation. She nodded emphatically.

"As curious as I am, we've got a lot on our plates and it's our summer vacation. We should be having fun, right?" she said.

"Hear, hear!" said Phyllis, raising her glass of wine and motioning for them to raise their glasses of sweet tea. "To an unforgettable summer of fun and sun!" she exclaimed.

They clinked their glasses and resumed their meal.

After dinner, as promised, Phyllis went to Devlin's room to survey his wardrobe armed with a pen and pad. Lola did not join them, preferring to check her messages, both texts, and emails, since no phones were allowed at the dinner table and she hadn't had time to check her phone all day.

She was in her alcove reading the back-and-forth replies about Tom's party on the app her friends used to communicate. Tom had apparently posed a question before leaving on vacation and had added Lola and Devlin to the conversation. She'd seen the link in her emails but hadn't known what it was until Sara asked why she wasn't on the app. So she downloaded it, logged on, and joined the conversation. Or tried to follow the feed that had been going on for the last three days. The initial question had been:

Please choose one of the following themes and say why it's your favorite or how we could best exploit it. 1-1920s Speakeasies 2-Disco Inferno 3-Casino Royale.

So far, the most popular theme was 1920s Speakeasies. Lola saw that Devlin had responded last night. He liked the Casino Royale theme because he was good at poker. Lola voted for Disco Inferno because she loved the music, the bellbottoms, and who didn't like a disco ball!

She hadn't heard the knock on the door, so she nearly fell off her chair when she heard Phyllis at the bottom of the corkscrew staircase calling up to her.

"Phyllis, you scared me! I didn't hear you come in," she said, coming down the stairs.

"I'm sorry, darling. I only came in to say goodnight and to see if you needed anything on tomorrow's shopping expedition," she said, turning towards the closet.

Lola followed her in. "I really don't think so. You bought me clothes for just about every occasion. We might need to do a quick trip next week for Tom's party. I just saw the proposed themes and I'm not equipped for any of those!" she said, rattling off the choices.

"I have got you covered, darling. I've got something amazing for every one of those themes in my wardrobe. Don't you fret! And if those don't suit the theme, we'll have Madame Beaufort whip something up just for you," said Phyllis.

Phyllis selected the items Lola should bring for the house party and hung them together on one of the rails. Then deciding Lola had everything she needed, she kissed her cheek and said goodnight.

Lola returned to her emails and wrote back to Jane and Sara, then shut off her laptop and went to get ready for bed.

21

MARBLE

She had just finished brushing her teeth when she heard a shout in her head. *Lola, come here!* Devlin sounded excited, or scared. *Where are you?* She figured he was in his room, but it didn't hurt to ask. *In my room, come quickly.*

She put on her slippers and dashed to his room, giving a cursory knock before entering.

He was standing in front of his red door. He had his key in his right hand—she could see the chain dangling from it. But he was holding something else in his left hand.

"What it is? Did something happen at the Townhouse again?" she asked, walking briskly to him and peering into his hand. It was his marble.

"Look," he said, nodding towards the door.

She looked at the door and, at first, couldn't see what he was pointing at. But there it was. On the same side as the handle, a rectangle hollow in the door with some sort of socket in the center. It was about the size of a light switch; the socket was presumably for the marble.

Her jaw dropped open and she turned to him in astonishment

"So that's why your door is red! To distinguish it from regular trav-

110

eling doors. Did the socket appear when you held the marble?" she asked in fascination.

"Yes! I was looking for a book in my trunk and decide to open the wooden box to look at the letter and the marble. It was shimmering a little, as though it was willing me to pick it up. When I picked it up, I could feel it pulsing in my hand and power shot through my whole body. Did you feel that way when you picked up the watch?" he asked.

"It felt warm to the touch, but nothing like what you're describing. Then what happened?" she urged.

"I felt my key growing warm on my chest, so warm that I had to lift it off for fear it would burn me, but when I held the key in my hand, it was not hot. The door appeared and there was the socket," he said gesturing toward it.

"Should I open the door?" she asked mischievously.

"No! Yes! I don't know," he replied, unsure.

"Oh, come on. We'll just open it and flip through the options. What harm could that do?" said Lola, nodding vigorously, as though egging him on.

There was a knock at the door. Lola went to answer, opening it a mere crack to see who it was. But there was no one on the other side.

She came back and they heard the knock again. It was on the third knock that they realized it was coming from the red door.

"Who is it?" asked Lola in a tremulous voice.

"It is Headmaster Lianon. May I enter?" they heard from the other side of the door.

Lola was about to open the door, but Devlin stopped her.

"Wait. What if it's a trap, an impostor? Ask him something only he would know," suggested Devlin.

Lola thought for a minute. Then she smiled and asked, "What did you request I retrieve from my room when we were at the Academy?"

"Your copy of the Archives," he responded quickly.

Lola looked at Devlin and he nodded. He was still holding both his key and the marble like they were incendiary devices and a bomb would go off if he so much as moved an inch.

Lola turned the knob and pushed open the door. It opened into the

Headmaster's office, behind his desk. He was passing through his portal window. Lola moved out of the way to let him pass.

"Hello, children," he said, ducking under the doorjamb and into the room, closing the door behind him.

"I apologize for the late hour and the unannounced visit not only to your home, but it appears to your private quarters. But I was alerted when you accessed your socket. Could we perhaps put the marble in a safe place for the time being?" he asked, nodding to Devlin's hand.

Devlin lowered his arm slowly and turned to put the marble back in its box. The keypad disappeared. Then he put his key back around his neck and the door disappeared.

The Headmaster was looking around for somewhere to sit. Lola saw him eyeing the bistro set in front of the fire and suggested they go into her sitting room, next door.

He followed her out of Devlin's room and remarked on the lovely paintings hanging in the hall. Devlin brought up the rear.

Once they were settled, Devlin and Lola waited for the Headmaster to explain why he was here.

"World Jumpers are rare. At present, there are no more than ten in the world. It's hard to know exactly how many there are as the marbles are often lost when a World Jumper dies, only to resurface years later in the hands of a related Traveler. Anyhow, when a marble is used, it shows up on the world map in Summerset Isle, home of the Ancient and High Elves. When a marble that hadn't been used in a while is used, my brethren alert me to the location and I Travel there to investigate. In this instance, when I was given the coordinates, I knew exactly what was going on and hurried over before things went amiss," he explained.

Lola and Devlin exchanged a guilty look. "It was an accident," said Devlin, explaining how he came to hold both the key and the marble.

"We were only going to flip through the destinations," whispered Lola.

"Yes, I understand. It was an innocent folly," he said patiently. "But you see, when you 'flip through' as you say, you are in fact opening a portal, whether you cross into the world or not. Should a being in one of the worlds wish to exit, it could cross over into our world through the portal you have conveniently opened for them. Not all worlds are safe to cross to, and not all beings should be allowed out of their world, let alone into ours," he concluded.

"I see," said Devlin, looking at Lola who shivered, imagining a three-headed creature let loose in Williamsburg, Virginia because she just wanted to channel surf on the keypad.

"I'm very sorry, Headmaster. I honestly didn't know," she said contritely.

"That's alright. You didn't know. That's why we have a school. And that's unfortunately how many of the World Jumpers die, I'm afraid," he said with finality. Both Lola and Devlin looked contrite, heads bowed.

"On another note, I'm very concerned about the break-in at your Townhouse. I believe someone may have been looking for the marble or the pocket watch. You see, there are quite a few keyless Travelers around the world," he said.

At Lola's questioning look, he explained, "When a Traveler misuses their key, it may be revoked by his Custodian. If a Traveler breaks the rules of the Handbook, his key is revoked automatically and sent back to the Repository. If the key was revoked by the Custodian, it may be returned. But if the key was revoked magically, they become keyless Travelers. They retain the ability to Travel, it is their birthright. However, without a key, they cannot Travel on their own. They must Travel with another."

"What happens if a Custodian misuses his key?" asked Devlin.

"Any Traveler who witnesses or suspects the misuse of a key may submit a complaint to the Council of Elders. Underage Travelers may also submit a complaint to me, should the matter require some delicacy," he explained.

"So what happens to the keyless Travelers? What if they made a mistake or didn't know they were breaking the rules?" asked Lola, worried she might or her family might have broken the rules inadvertently.

"When a key is revoked magically, it is always with good reason and, since most Travelers have attended the Academy, they are usually well-schooled in the rules," he said. Then seeing Lola wringing her hands on her lap, if added, "If your father and aunt had broken the rules, their keys would have been revoked. Since your aunt is clearly still using hers, and your father used his until just recently, it is safe to say there has been no rule-breaking. You may relax, Lola."

"Now, most keyless Travelers will continue to Travel with a family member or a spouse and it usually isn't a problem. However, as you can imagine, there are a few bad apples here and there. They are unable to accept the loss of their key, their freedom, their power. Some will try to steal another Traveler's key, for example," he said.

Devlin's hand went straight to his key, patting it down to ensure it was still there.

"Can that really happen?" asked Devlin.

"It can, but the thief cannot use it more than once. Lost keys are immediately returned to the family's Repository. Should someone steal your key, it would turn up within twenty-four hours," he explained.

"How does the Custodian know that a key has been lost, returned, or even revoked?" asked Lola.

"This will all be covered extensively in the Custodian class at the Academy," replied the Headmaster. "Which of you will take on the duties?" he asked.

"I will," replied Devlin, sitting up straighter. The Headmaster inclined his head in acknowledgment.

"Suffice it to say, the Custodian will find out. As to whose key it is, your name was magically engraved on the body of the key," he said. Both Lola and Devlin reached for their keys and looked for the engraving. "It's invisible to the human eye," he said, chuckling at their confused faces. "You need to speak an incantation to reveal the name of the key bearer," he explained. He rose from his seat and hunched down over them. He waved his hands over the keys and the gold writing appeared on the keys for a moment and disappeared.

"Over the years, there have been various attempts to acquire keys, but most have failed. However, we have recently heard that a sorcerer of some sort has started recruiting keyless Travelers to form an alliance. It is rumored that he provides them with a way to Travel without keys," said the Headmaster, pacing now as though he were agitated.

"The break-in at the Townhouse was not an isolated event. Other Travelers have had break-ins, and it appears all of them owned either a pocket watch or a marble," he concluded.

"Were they stolen?" asked Devlin.

"No, thankfully the items were not on the premises at the time," he said. "They had been safely locked up in a vault at the Academy," said the Headmaster, staring pointedly at both of them.

"Is that what you want us to do? Hand over our artifacts for safe-keeping?" asked Lola.

"I would like you to discuss it as a family and give me an answer as soon as possible," he replied.

He rose and looked at each of them in turn and asked, "Can I trust that the marble will stay stowed in that box until the fall when it's time for proper instruction?"

"Yes, sir," answered Devlin.

"And you, young lady, can I trust you not to start turning dials on that pocket watch?" he asked Lola. Lola's eyes grew wide. "Yes, I know you found the watch. It too is tracked in Summerset, though it's harder to pinpoint a specific watch and where it's being used," he explained.

"Yes, sir," replied Lola.

"Very well. I'll await your decision on the artifacts. Should you decide to leave them with the Academy, we'll arrange a time for the safe transfer. Otherwise, I'll see you in three weeks!" he said.

He surveyed the room and walked around the sofa to stand in front of the massive fireplace. Lola and Devlin rose and turned to observe him.

He waved in the air and the huge round window appeared. There was a shimmer, but they could clearly see his office on the other side of it. He stepped through the shimmer. It was more like a mist than a ripple of water, like Lola had seen in movies.

"Headmaster," she cried and he turned to look at her. "Don't you have a marble or a socket?" she asked.

"Of course not, I'm a High Elf!" he exclaimed, and with a wave of the hand, the portal disappeared.

22

CHANGE

The next morning at breakfast, Lola and Devlin recounted their encounter with the Headmaster to Phyllis.

"Oh my. Can you just imagine unleashing some otherworldly monstrosity into our peaceful county!" she said, fanning herself and shuddering at the thought. "It was a close call."

"Which is why I think it's best if we take our time with the Archives and everything. We should stick to regular Traveling and practicing the incantations we have learned to make it safer," said Devlin. "Our Ancestor was unusual at the very least, and his association with a witch clearly makes us a different kind of Traveler. I believe that should come with an extra set of responsibilities," he concluded.

"I couldn't have said it any better, Devlin. How mature you are for your age," said Phyllis.

"Obviously I'm not as mature since it was my idea to start checking out the world catalog," said Lola with a pout.

"The important thing is nothing happened and that you both learned from the experience. I admit that even I feel somewhat chastised. First for the fact that Simon and I traveled to our hearts' content, oblivious of any safety procedures or incantations. We were pretty much given a key and told not to get caught using it," she said with a laugh. "Although, come to think of it, the situation is rather similar to driving a car. When we were young, a family member showed you how to drive and you drove. There were no lessons and permits and certainly no laws about seat belts and the like. And we turned out just fine," she said.

"That's true, a lot of things are more complicated now. Probably because there are more people to contend with," said Lola. "All I know is that I don't want to get in trouble with the Academy. I really like the school, I like my friends, I like my room, and I really, really like the food there," she added emphatically.

She was so earnest that Phyllis and Devlin both burst out laughing.

"Why are people always laughing at me!" she said, trying hard not to stamp her foot like a petulant child as she said it.

"We are not laughing at you, Lola. It is only that you are so spontaneous and adorable. It is a joy to see, and so we laugh," replied Devlin. Lola was somewhat mollified. To change the subject, she asked what they were going to do about the artifacts.

"Should we keep them here? Send them to the Radcliff's vault? Send them to the Academy?" she asked.

"The Archives and the Repository have always been safe in their vault, and Devlin can easily call them back. I don't know that it would be so easy if they were at the Academy. It's in a different world," said Phyllis.

"I agree. As safe as the Academy seems, I would feel better knowing exactly where the artifacts are and have access to them should we need them," put in Devlin.

"Well, I agree they can't stay here. No matter how sophisticated our security system is, it's no match for magic," said Lola. "But I think we should test the theory. Devlin, call the pocket watch."

Devlin closed his eyes and took a deep breath. He put out his hand to receive it and spoke, "Bring me the pocket watch." The timepiece appeared in his hand.

"Now send it to the Vault. Then, do the same with the Archives and the marble," she suggested.

"Also try to call the Repository from the Vault," put in Phyllis.

Devlin called the marble and when it arrived, he sent it to the Vault. He called the Archives and sent it to the Vault as well. Then he called the Repository. He had never seen it before. Before sending it back, he opened it and saw it contained twelve slots. Four of the keys were missing. He frowned.

"If the three of us have keys, who has the fourth key?" he asked, turning the small wood chest so Phyllis and Lola could see.

They looked at each other, then back at him.

"I don't know. Perhaps a key was lost over the years," suggested Phyllis.

"But the Headmaster told us lost, stolen, or revoked keys are magically returned to the Repository," explained Lola.

They sat there, quietly caught up in their respective thoughts.

"What if it's Dad's key?" said Lola, tentatively. "I mean he just disappeared on my sixteenth birthday and there was no explanation. Then the pocket watch appears in his room out of nowhere. If he was dead, his key would have returned to the Repository," she ventured.

Phyllis swallowed audibly. Twice she opened her mouth to speak, but nothing came out.

Devlin was still frowning, clearly mulling over something in his mind.

"Mother said in her letter that the box containing the key and the marble appeared out of nowhere when I was thirteen. We were told at school that thirteen is the age when Travelers receive their keys. We were also told that, though it was rare, keys have appeared out of nowhere to other children whose parents had died before they could explain or who hadn't known their parents were Travelers. The explanation seemed to apply to my situation, and I did not question it further. But now I wonder. How did the box arrive at my home? If it was magic, how would it know to give me the marble as well? Where was it before it came to me? If the key inside the box is an Evers key, someone would have needed to remove it from the Repository and place it in the box I received. Where was the marble before it came to me?" said Devlin, more to himself than anybody else.

"We should ask Mr. Radcliff. I'll need to call him to have him check the Vault for the items you sent. Why don't you send the Repository back now?" suggested Phyllis.

"Before you do, just to be on the safe side, call back the watch, the marble, and the book," suggested Lola.

Devlin squared his shoulders and sighed. His patience was wearing thin with their requests, but he tamped down on his temper since he knew they were right. He called back all three items. Now everything was set before him on the table.

"Do you think there are other artifacts in the vault?" he asked now, puzzled. "I would like the entire contents of the vault," he tried.

A banker's box titled *Evers' paperwork* appeared as well as a scroll. The box held current titles and deeds. The scroll was their family tree. He gave it a quick glance and sent everything back. He put his hands on the table, pushed back his chair, and rose.

"My head hurts and I need a little time to process all of this," said Devlin on an exhale. "If you will excuse me, ladies, I believe Jackson is waiting for me in the Library. Hopefully, the attorney will get back to us quickly and we'll know more at lunchtime," he said and left the room.

Lola and Phyllis waited until Devlin had left the room before resuming the conversation. "I think this whole Custodian business is a little more than he bargained for. I hope he's not going to change his mind because I know how he feels and I don't want to be in his shoes!" said Lola nervously.

"He's just a little overwhelmed. Men need to let things sit for a while. He'll be fine," replied Phyllis. Changing the subject, Lola asked where they were conducting the interviews and how they would proceed.

"I thought it would be nice to have them out on the patio. I find everyone is nervous in those situations, and being outside with a pitcher of sweet tea feels more relaxed. Also, we won't be in Marie's way, but she can still see and hear what's going on. Her indirect input will be helpful. She knows a lot of people in the area, and likely knows more about the job than we do!" said Phyllis.

Lola nodded. "At what time does the first couple arrive?" she asked.

Phyllis checked her watch. "Right about now, we better get a move on!"

The interviews went well. Lola liked the second couple, John and Sally, best. When the last couple had gone, Phyllis asked Marie to come and sit with them and give her impressions. She had nothing bad to say about the first couple, but she obviously didn't favor them. About the third couple, she had heard they had been let go for not living up to their employer's expectations, though she did not provide further details. If it was up to her, she'd pick John and Sally.

"Me too!" said Lola, excitedly.

"Me three!" said Phyllis, laughing. "Well, that was much easier than anticipated. Well done, ladies!" she exclaimed, and they toasted to their new hires.

"Should I let them stew over the weekend, or call them this after-noon?" she asked wickedly.

"Stop your jesting," chided Marie. "I want them here at seven on Monday morning! We've got a lot of ground to cover and I'm looking forward to that trip you promised me, Ms. Phyllis!" said Marie, waving her off like it was a bunch of nonsense.

"Yes, ma'am," replied Phyllis as she got up. "I'll call them right away," she said over her shoulder as she went inside.

Marie followed her in and went on with her tasks.

Checking her watch, Lola went in after them to see what was avail-able for lunch. The boys were still in the Library, and Phyllis hadn't indicated if she was coming back for lunch. However, she had said they were going shopping after lunch, so people were bound to show up sooner or later.

"Marie, what can I make for lunch?" Lola asked.

"Just you or the lot of you?" asked Marie.

"Everyone, you too if you want," said Lola.

"I've got some chicken salad ready. Come give me a hand and we'll make some sandwiches for everyone," she replied.

"Okay, what do I do first?" asked Lola.

"Well, you start by washing your hands. Then get some plates and get the bread. I made two loaves this morning, they're in the bread box," replied the cook, pointing at the box in the corner by the window. She took out a bread knife, the one with a slicing guide, and a wooden chopping board. When Lola was done, she showed her how to make perfect slices with the guide.

"When you've practiced some, you'll be able to slice the bread without the guide," she said, getting an ice cream scoop and placing a scoop of chicken salad on the slices as Lola put them on the plates. Once each plate had two slices and a scoop. She spread it filling with a knife and had Lola top each one with a leaf of lettuce and a couple of sliced tomatoes. Finally, they cranked out some sea salt and black pepper, closed the sandwiches, and sliced them in half crosswise.

Marie took out a container of carrot and apple slaw she had prepared and had Lola add a heap of it to all the plates. The finishing touch was a handful of plain kettle chips. Marie got a fresh pitcher of sweet tea out of the icebox and voilà, lunch was ready.

"Thanks for your help, Lola," said Marie.

"I think I'm the one who should be thanking you," replied Lola with a laugh, though she was beaming with pride.

When Phyllis came in and saw all the plates with their contents ready to eat, Marie said, "Guess who made lunch today?"

Phyllis smiled and looked at Lola, impressed. "Did you make this for us, Lola?"

"I helped Marie," she said, looking down a little bashfully.

"It was her idea and all I did was give her a hand and a few pointers!" replied Marie.

The women took the food outside on the patio table and were soon joined by the men.

They had a nice lunch and discussed the arrival of the new couple on Monday.

"Jackson, you'll be on hand to show John around and provide him with a list of duties, security codes, and the like?" asked Phyllis.

"Yes, of course. I've got everything set up," he replied.

"How long do you think they'll need to train for before being let loose?" Phyllis asked both Marie and Jackson. Devlin and Lola kept eating and just listened.

"I think three days to follow me around, then two days of her doing everything and me supervising and providing feedback should do the trick," said Marie.

"That sounds about right. I'll only provide security codes on Friday to be sure they are both doing satisfactorily. Have they both been cleared by the attorney?" he asked Phyllis.

"Yes, references were checked and they passed the background check," she answered.

"Will they be moving into the cottage?" asked Lola.

"At the end of the week, if we decide to hire them, yes. They'll move in next weekend," she replied. "Is that okay with you, Jackson?" she asked.

"Yes, of course. Everything is ready. If you meant because of my parents, other than the general structure, the cottage doesn't look anything like the home it was with my parents. All of those memories are in here," he said, tapping his temple. "Not out there," he added.

"It's time someone lived in the cottage and it's time the Mansion had a full staff to take care of it. No offense to you, Marie," he said.

She smiled and replied, "None taken, I agree!"

He took a sip of his tea and continued his impassioned speech. "More people are living here, now. It's not just Phyllis anymore and, hopefully, there will be more and more entertaining and liveliness in the house again," he concluded. Then he smiled shyly, realizing he'd gotten a little carried away.

"Hear, hear!" said Devlin, raising his glass. "To new beginnings for everyone at this table!" he said, and they all clinked glasses.

"Indeed! A new school for Jackson, Devlin, and Lola in the fall," said Phyllis.

"A new retired lifestyle for Marie," said Lola.

"And a long vacation!" added Phyllis, winking at Marie.

"A long vacation for me too!" said Jackson, rubbing his hands in anticipation.

"A newish romance for Phyllis?" quipped Lola, nudging her aunt with her elbow. Phyllis blushed but nodded her head vigorously.

"And a new family for me!" said Devlin, throwing his arms wide as though to encompass them all. He was grinning from ear to ear and looked so happy that everyone said, "Hear, hear!" and clinked their glasses again.

When lunch was over, they all pitched in to clean up and do the dishes while Marie went to finish up the laundry.

23

SURPRISE

When it was time to go shopping, Lola decided to opt-out and spend the afternoon by the pool. With the dinner party that night and the house party the next day, she felt like she needed a little preventative alone-time.

Devlin and Phyllis set off together, and Lola promised not to do any magic-related research in their absence. Instead, she grabbed her book, and her goggles headed for the pool. She was blissfully alone. Jackson had driven Phyllis and Devlin into Williamsburg so he could give Devlin some pointers on driving the Bentley. If things went well, Devlin would drive Phyllis and Lola to the house party and Jackson would get the weekend off.

Marie was in the kitchen, finishing up the preparations for the night's dinner party, and she too would be off for the weekend.

Lola did some laps, then sank face down into the lounge chair and fell asleep. A little while later, she flipped over onto her back, refreshed from her nap. She was reading her book when she got a very odd feeling like the air had changed, though there was no breeze and she didn't smell anything strange. It was a warm July day, but the hair on her arms rose. She was staring dumbly at it when she heard someone yell, "Surprise!"

She jumped at the sound and looked up, confused. It was Sara, walking through a door.

"Sara?" asked Lola, completely bewildered.

"Lola! It's me. I'm here!" she said, crossing over to her friend and standing expectantly at the end of her chair. Lola had stared as she approached, and now just looked up at her. Then, shaking herself, she got up and hugged her friend.

"I can't believe you're here," she said, laughing. "I mean I know how you got here, but I just don't believe it!" she said. "It's like everything that happened at school was completely removed from life here in Virginia," she said, still amazed.

"But you're here! What a lovely surprise!" she said, recovering. "Can I get you a bottle of water?" she asked, remembering her manners. "Can you stay? Did you bring your bathing suit?" she asked.

Sara laughed and said, "There she is! You seemed utterly speechless there for a minute, I was worried!" She sat in the chair opposite Lola. "I can stay for a bit. I tried to phone you before I came, but you didn't pick up," she explained.

"I left my phone in my room, sorry!"

"No worries. Then I popped in and rang the doorbell, but there was no answer," she laughed. "Then I remembered you said you had a pool. But you were asleep, so I've been checking the window every few minutes until I could see you were awake. I didn't want to give you a fright. And by the look on your face just then, I now realize you don't like surprises!" she said with a chuckle.

"Of course I do. Everyone likes surprises!" rebuffed Lola.

"It's perfectly fine. I'll make sure to make firm plans with you next time. It's only I was free for a couple of hours and figured you might be too. And here we are!" she said, placing her hands on her lap.

"Do you want to go and get your bathing suit? We have a bunch of new ones in the pool house if you don't want to bother," said Lola.

"Yes, I think I will. The weather is lovely here! Much warmer than at home. Give me five minutes and I'll pop right back," said Sara, getting up from the lounge chair. She took out her key and opened the door, then turned to Lola and said, "Do you want to have a quick peek at my room? You could hold the door while I get my swim trunks."

Lola shrugged and got up. She went to stand next to her friend. Sara turned the knob and held the door open for Lola.

Lola leaned on the doorjamb. It was nighttime in Gloucester and there was only a faint light on in Sara's bedroom. As she moved about the room, she switched on the overhead light and the room was bathed in bright light. Sara's room looked exactly like Lola had pictured it: a slanted roof with old wood windows on either side of her double bed. The windows were deep, and the sills were fitted with comfy cushions to turn them into window seats.

The bed itself had to be an antique. It was a wrought-iron four-poster bed with frilly drapes all around it. Lola recognized the bedspread from their dorm room. Lola couldn't see the rest of the room without closing the door, and she wasn't mentally ready to actually be in England just now. Besides, Sara was done and heading back to the door. She crossed back and closed the door. Lola showed Sara where she could change and grab a towel if she needed one.

When she came back, they went to sit on the side of the pool and put their feet in.

"Did you put some sunscreen on?" Lola asked her friend. When she shook her head, Lola got up and gave her the tube. "You're even paler than I am. Apply liberally. I'll do your back," she suggested.

"Thanks. Can you imagine I went home with a sunburn at night! My parents would know I was up to no good!" she chuckled.

"Your parents don't know you're here? Where do they think you are?" asked Lola, finishing up Sara's back. She gave her the tube and asked Sara to do hers.

"They think I've gone to my room. I'm going out later with friends. Regular human friends. Don't worry, they're used to it," she replied, and she gave the tube of sunscreen back to Lola. "There, we're both safe from the sun's harsh rays, can we go in the pool now, Mum?" quipped Sara.

Lola laughed and replied, "Of course! It's the first time I've been accused of being the mature, responsible one," and they jumped into the pool. They splashed around like eight-years-olds for a while, then sat down in the corner steps, facing the sun.

"You won't believe what happened yesterday," said Lola.

"What?" asked Sara, excited by her friend's tone of voice.

"The Headmaster barged into Devlin's room last night!" she said looking at Sara with huge eyes for emphasis.

"You're pulling my leg," scoffed Sara.

"No, I'm not. But I am exaggerating for effect. He actually knocked," said Lola and went on to explain the whole story to Sara, including finding the pocket watch. She left out the bits about the Archives since she knew no one other than the school was supposed to have a copy.

"That's incredible!" she exclaimed. "You're so lucky to be special Travelers," she added.

"We've barely mastered basic Traveling as it is. We're not ready for anything fancy yet," said Lola. "Let's talk about something else. Tell me about tonight. Where are you going, who will be there, and what kind of mischief will you get into?"

That topic kept them busy for a good long time. Then they moved on to boys, and finally to Tom's party.

"I can't believe it's next weekend already," said Lola.

"I know! I thought I'd miss you and Devlin and the gang terribly. But it's been family outings and parties all week at home. And more of the same next week," she said.

They heard voices in the distance and turned towards the sound. The shoppers had returned. Phyllis was shading her eyes, trying to figure out who was with Lola. Devlin must have recognized Sara and told her who it was. She waved at them and Jackson, arms loaded with packages and bags, gave a chin nod and followed Phyllis into the house through the mudroom. Devlin set his bags by the door and strode quickly towards them. It was all he could do not to run, but he had some dignity.

"Hi, Sara!" he said, waving at her from beyond the gate. She waved back and they lost sight of him as he went around through the pool house and onto the pool deck. He made a beeline for the pool and stopped at the edge.

"It is so good to see you. What a lovely surprise!" he said, beaming down at her. Turning, he went to fetch a towel and came back to hold it out for her. Sara looked at Lola and then got out of the pool. Devlin wrapped her in the towel and wrapped his arms around her tightly. "I've missed you," he said, kissing her cheek and letting her go. As Lola exited the pool, he rushed over to get her towel and held it out to her. She gave him a look and yanked it out of his hands. She wrapped it around herself, but she said, "Thanks," as she passed him and they went to sit in the lounge chairs to dry off.

"What are you doing here? Is this why you didn't come shopping with us, Lola?" asked Devlin.

"No, it was a total surprise!" replied Lola.

"It was a spur-of-the-moment decision. You should have seen her face, Devlin. She was utterly shocked to see me here," said Sara.

"Yes, I can imagine. Lola likes things to be planned in advance," he said, trying to suppress a smile.

"You say that like I'm incapable of doing anything spontaneous. Really, you two. I can roll with it, I swear!" said Lola.

They only smiled at her and Devlin changed the subject.

"Lola, I'm sorry to be a party pooper, but it's past five and we need to get ready for our guests," he said.

"Already?" she asked in surprise.

"Oh dear, I've got to run! My friends will wonder where I am and my mum doesn't like me to leave home so late to go out. She thinks it's indecent that I leave right when she's off to bed, so I make a point of lounging with my parents a bit before I head out," she said with a laugh. She grabbed her things off the table, blew them each a kiss and was through her door in a flash. They stared at the space where her door had vanished for a few seconds, then at each other.

"Alrighty, then. Let's get ready for our dinner party," said Lola, rising from her chair and getting her things together.

24

VACATION

The weekend was a total blur. The dinner party was a success, and Devlin was a hit with Matthew and Sheila. And they all had a blast at the house party. Just before they had left, an extra passenger appeared on their doorstep: Boris. Phyllis and Boris sat in the back, giggling like teenagers while Lola sat upfront with Devlin, who was thrilled to be driving the Bentley. Once at the massive beach house, the parents had gone one way, and the teenagers were taken in an entirely different direction. The whole upper floor had been dedicated to the younger crowd. Four huge bedrooms that could each sleep four to eight people in the same double-sized bunk beds as they had at home. Lola and Devlin had claimed a set by throwing their bags on the bunks, then gotten their bathing suits and headed for the beach.

The Mansion had its own private beach. They had so many chairs and parasols it looked like an exclusive beachfront resort more than a single-family home.

There was a beach bar for drinks and snacks. There were paddleboards, surfboards, sea kayaks, jet skis. There was even a lifeguard.

Most of the adults had stayed by the massive pool. Once in a while, Lola could see Phyllis' huge lavender hat pop up to check on her and Devlin.

Devlin played beach volleyball with a bunch of people he just met. Lola lay in a covered cabana, sipping mocktails and reading her book. *This was the life*, Lola thought. It was the perfect distraction to the whole magic situation and from imagining her father was still alive, somewhere.

Dinner and the bonfire were a lot of fun, and there had been very little sleeping. Despite air conditioning blasting in the rooms, the rooms still felt hot and stuffy, packed as they were with kids ranging from twelve to twenty years of age.

At brunch the next day, everyone was tired and subdued, ready to go home.

On the ride back, Phyllis asked them to make a list of places they would like to see. They would take the next five days to Travel as a family. Either to multiple destinations or many days in one location. She promised to be back well in time for Tom's party and to make any preparations that might be required.

"I'm really at a loss to come up with places to visit. I've never been anywhere," said Lola.

"I have mostly visited European cities near our home with Mother, I would like to see places in nature. Mountains, fields of flowers, beaches, or maybe some light hiking," replied Devlin.

"Oh, could we go to Disney World?" asked Lola, grinning like a kid.

Phyllis and Boris chuckled in the back.

"When we get home, we should all get a bit of rest. Give it some thought and we can discuss it further at dinner. If you still can't decide, I'll narrow down some choices. We have a few other apartments in addition to the one in Florence," she said.

"And we have a few as well," interjected Boris. "You are welcome to use any of our homes that are not currently in use," he offered.

"That's very kind of you, Boris," said Lola.

"Thank you, sir," replied Devlin.

Once they got home, they said goodbye to Boris and each of them went to their respective rooms for a much-needed nap.

※—※

When she woke up from her nap, Lola had a shower and went to check her email. Tom had sent the final instructions for the party, which was to be on the Saturday. People could arrive as early as eleven, but no later than three p.m. The party would end no earlier than three p.m. on Sunday and departure was expected to be before five p.m. Lola and Devlin would be back in time for the family dinner.

The chosen theme was the 20s Speakeasy with a twist: It was going to be a murder-mystery evening. Apparently, Tom's uncle was a famous screenwriter. He had been with them on vacation and offered to write a script for Tom and his friends to act out. Since he was going to be living with them for a few months, he would be on hand to help out. He also had a lot of contacts in the film and theater industry, so guests should prepare to be amazed.

Each of them would receive their part via Traveling letter by Wednesday. A list of characters would be emailed later in the week so that everyone knew who everybody was. At present, there were about twenty confirmed guests. Any special requests were to be emailed before noon on Monday.

No gifts were requested or desired. Parental supervision would be provided by Tom's mother and her brother. The email also gave a general schedule for the event, directions on where to arrive by door, and a list of suggested items to bring.

Lola was very excited and couldn't wait to receive her part. She went down to dinner earlier to help Phyllis out and tell her about the party theme before Jackson arrived. It turned out there was no need as Jackson wouldn't be joining them for dinner. He was away for the weekend and would be home in time for work on Monday morning.

"What a fantastic theme for a party!" exclaimed Phyllis. "I have a lot of things from the twenties. This will be such fun!" she said with enthusiasm. They were having drinks on the porch that night.

"I have never been to such a party. I am a little nervous," admitted Devlin.

"You did marvelously on Friday night and over the weekend, sugar. Don't you worry about a thing. In the twenties, all the men dressed the same, so wardrobe won't be an issue. And since I'm not attending the party, and I can keep a secret, I can help you both with your parts," she said reassuringly.

They moved their discussion to the dining room. Tonight they were having a tuna casserole that Phyllis had defrosted when they arrived and put in the oven upon waking from her nap. She'd also defrosted some dinner rolls and a cherry cobbler. Lola and Devlin thought it was delicious and wouldn't have known she hadn't spent the entire afternoon slaving in the kitchen.

"Now that we're alone. I'd like to discuss Simon, the missing key, and what the attorneys had to say about my marble. You never did get a chance to tell us what he said," said Devlin.

"That's right," said Phyllis, putting down her fork and composing herself. "Edward said he doesn't know anything about the box or the marble and he has never seen inside the Repository so he was unable to say how many keys were in it at any time. He asked his father, and he didn't know about it either."

Lola and Devlin stopped eating and put their forks down. The implication was undeniable. Only one person could have sent Devlin the key and the marble. Simon. And that implied that Simon had found out about Devlin.

"It looks like you are not the only one who can keep a secret," said Devlin, brooding.

"If Simon knew about Devlin, why didn't he tell me?" asked Phyllis, mostly to herself.

"Why didn't he reach out to Devlin?" asked Lola, voicing the words she imagined Devlin himself was thinking, though she could not currently hear his thoughts.

"If he is alive, where is he now?" asked Devlin.

So many questions and so few answers. Lola's eyebrows shot up, and she slapped her hand on the table.

"What if it wasn't Dad who sent the key and the marble? What if the key and marble that Devlin has didn't come from an Evers?" she said, eyes huge.

"How would that even work? It would have to be an Evers key, or it wouldn't function," said Phyllis, confused at where this was going. "Unless his mother came from a family of Travelers," she said.

"Take out your keys, let's compare them," said Lola, removing her ribbon from around her neck and putting her key in the center of the table.

Deciding to indulge her, both Phyllis and Devlin produced their keys and placed them near Lola's. All three keys were identical skeleton keys.

"Okay, so they are the same. But, Devlin, did you notice that the keys our friends have were different? They looked like regular old metal keys. They weren't skeleton keys. When I asked about it, I was told it was because I was a Time Walker. I figured it meant I could open doors differently. But then the watch appeared, and it made more sense. Do you think you could call the book and we could ask it all these questions?" she suggested.

"Why don't we finish eating and take this discussion to the Library. I think we might need to take notes or draw a list of more questions," proposed Phyllis.

"I'm not hungry anymore," said Lola.

"Neither am I," replied Devlin.

"To be honest, I'm not very hungry anymore either. Let's just put all this in the kitchen. Who knows, our appetites might come back once we get to the bottom of this," she said, cheerily.

25

SPHERE

In the Library, Lola and Phyllis sat in the armchairs, and Devlin took the desk. He called the book and waited before asking his first question.

"Perhaps we should ask the book about the marble first," suggested Phyllis.

Devlin nodded and asked the book to tell them about the marble. The book opened to a section called *World Jumping*. It was an index of sorts; there were two subsections titled *Generalities* and *Instructions*. Devlin flipped to the first section and blanched. There were pages upon pages of *Generalities*. There was no way he was reading all of this out loud. He tapped a finger on his upper lip and spoke, "Archive, can you summarize the origins, purpose, and use of the marble?"

Lola cocked her head and stared at the book, wondering what it would do and half expected it to speak. It didn't speak, but turned to a blank section page and wrote out a response:

"First, the object in question is not marble. Marbles are toys created in Germany in the 1800s. The artifact used to access other worlds is in fact a Sphere crafted from Nuummite, often referred to as the Sorcerer's Stone. Mined exclusively in Greenland, Nuummite was formed from a volcanic eruption around 3.8 billion years ago, making it one of the oldest stones on earth.

Nuummite vibrates at its own frequency, emitting what is called piezoelectricity, an electrical charge that is released from crystals once they are pressed or cut.

It has been known to store unlimited amounts of information. Because of these properties, it was chosen as an anchor for World Jumpers. Not only can it receive the transmission of thought from a Traveler and register their intended destination, but it will also retain their current coordinates and will do so for each Jump. All Nuummite Spheres are interconnected and gather collective knowledge. Hence, any of the Spheres will hold the knowledge gathered by all Spheres for all voyages ever completed or attempted.

The High Elves gifted each of the original twelve Elders with a Nuummite Sphere so that they may study other worlds and learn from them. The Sphere, or marble as it was later termed, would pass to his successor once he died. Details of its current use within the Traveler Community are unknown by your Ancestors. However, our family's Nuummite Sphere can still access the collective knowledge. Archibald did not initially use the Sphere, for fear it would lead his former colleagues directly to him, should they find out he had made off with a copy of the Archivum and wish to retaliate. He put it away for safe-keeping and never told anyone about it, not even his wife. When he died, the marble was lost.

As to its use, if the Traveler knows where he would like to go, he should communicate it to the Sphere, verbally or telepathically, while holding it. Then, he should place it in the socket so the Sphere may input coordinates of the destination and then those to return to. Once this is completed, it will glow. The Traveler may simply pocket the marble and open his door. On the other hand, if the Traveler is open to suggestions, he may provide some requirements to his Sphere before taking out his key. This will ensure that only safe locations corre-sponding to the Traveler's requirements will be offered. The marble will become very warm to the touch when it is ready to be used. Then, and only then, should the Traveler take out his key and place the marble in the socket. The Traveler should say the incantation to render the door transparent and roll the marble within the socket to switch from one proposed location to the next until he has reviewed all selections. Once he has made his choice, he should remove his hand from the marble and wait for it to glow before pocketing it and opening his door."

"Wow," said Lola. "So where did your marble come from? Who gave it to you?" she wondered aloud.

"Archive, are you saying the Evers marble has never been used before?" he asked the book.

"The Evers Sphere was never used by Archibald Evers. Two of his Descendants have used it."

"Who used the marble?" asked Devlin.

"Simon Evers and Devlin Evers."

Phyllis and Lola gasped. "Does it even count if you didn't actually open a door?" asked Lola.

"If he touched the marble, the Nuummite registered it; it certainly showed up on the High Elves' radar," replied Phyllis.

Devlin needed answers. "When did Simon Evers use it?" he asked.

"We are unable to answer that question."

Devlin tried something else. "Where did Simon Evers go?"

"We are unable to answer that question."

Devlin sighed and pushed away from the desk. He got up and started walking around, shaking out his limbs as though trying to shake away his impatience.

"If we want to know when and where it was used, we will have to ask the Headmaster. But now I think I understand why he was so adamant that we leave our artifacts at the Academy for safekeeping," he said, combing his fingers through his hair.

Lola looked up at him, catching on to his thread of thought.

"Evers have been flying under the Academy's radar for generations. I have a feeling the watch hadn't been used either until Dad used it. And that's how the Academy found out about us. It tracked the watch here, to this house, and found a Traveler: Me. It tracked the marble to Sweden and found another Traveler: Devlin. Boom, instant admission letters to the Academy. Then there's an investigation into our sudden appearance in the Traveler Community, and into our mothers' deaths. Boom: we're related. Then I tell them that Dad traveled through time to see me and now they want our artifacts," said Lola, crossing her arms like a lawyer resting her case.

"They say it's to avoid them falling into the wrong hands. You don't think that would include us, do you?" asked Phyllis, sitting up straighter in her chair. "This certainly explains why there were no Evers on the Council. Boris thought that was strange. He figured it was because we were Americans and there was a different Council for the Americas."

Now Lola was frowning. "But when Dad summoned the Council, wasn't there another American Traveler and a Canadian as well? Why did it summon *that* Council, the one Boris' family was on? The book told us there were multiple Councils around the world. Why not have a Council on this continent?" she asked.

"Perhaps because the emergency, my kidnapping, involved one of the families on that Council," suggested Phyllis. Lola nodded, it made sense.

Devlin was pacing now, rubbing his forehead in consternation. He sat back down and stared at the book.

"Is Simon Evers alive?" he asked the book.

"We are unable to answer that question."

"This is so frustrating!" cried Devlin, waving his hands in the air.

"Why do you think the book responds that way?" asked Lola, shifting in her seat to sit cross-legged.

"Perhaps because he has used both the watch and the marble, the book is unable to pinpoint where he is in space and time," suggested Phyllis, getting up to pour herself a bit of brandy and leaning on the window sill as she drank it.

"Yes, that makes sense," replied Devlin, calming down a little.

"Okay. We know for a fact that Dad used the watch to time travel so he could meet me. To pinpoint when I would arrive here, he may have had to Travel ahead to various points in time," said Lola, getting up now and started to walk around as she did when she was getting excited about an idea. "What if he popped in later and saw Devlin here? That would have thrown him for a loop, and he would have wanted to investigate it. Once he was sure Devlin was his son, he could easily have gone back in time to deliver the box with the key and marble. If people are looking for the marble, what better hiding place than in the past!" said Lola, on a roll now.

"But where did he get the marble from?" asked Phyllis.

"Perhaps he went back in time and met with Archibald. Archibald could have given him the marble for safekeeping. For Archibald, having the artifacts safe in the future would ensure that could not be used to track him down," mused Devlin.

"Exactly!" exclaimed Lola, giddy now at the prospect that she might yet see her father again.

"He did spend a lot of time researching while he was sick, and he may have been Traveling when I thought he was resting," conceded Phyllis.

"If he was able to Travel far enough into the future, he could have found a cure for cancer and taken it," said Lola hopefully.

"But how would that work? I remember him dying; it was awful. If he had managed to cure himself and not die, wouldn't my memory of the events have changed, whether I was aware of the change or not?" asked Phyllis, pinching the top of her nose.

"What if he faked his own death and has been Traveling through time trying to figure out how to make his comeback?" said Lola.

"Right, but now we have the watch," replied Devlin.

"We have the watch and the marble. Yet, there is still a key missing. That has to mean that Dad is here. In *this* time," said Lola excitedly. "Maybe he dropped the watch accidentally and couldn't retrieve it because Marie came into the room," she offered.

"But why wouldn't he come to me, or leave a note," said Phyllis. "Lola, you have no idea how much I want my brother back, but it feels like we're grasping at straws here," she added.

"I would love to meet my father, and if it is at all possible, I think we have to look into every possible scenario, no matter how unlikely," said Devlin, getting up to stand near Lola, as though to show a united front.

"You have been spending a lot of time with Boris, Phyllis. Father may have tried to connect with you and couldn't catch you alone. None of us has been spending much time on our own since coming back from school," said Devlin, warming up to the idea more and more.

"What if he is here, in this time, and has been Traveling from house to house to avoid being seen? You said we have multiple homes around the world. It would be easy for him to do," he said.

"Yes! And from what the Headmaster told us, I think it's safe to say we are being watched. If not by the Academy, then by whoever is looking for the watch and marble. Also, he may have dropped the watch by accident, intending to get it back, but it was gone when he came back for it," said Lola. "Do you think we should put it back? And maybe check to see if he takes it?"

"We'd have no way to know for sure he took it," said Phyllis. "No, I think we should leave him a note in his room, and send the same note to each of our homes, just in case."

"But what if the people who ransacked the Townhouse try to break into the other homes? What if they already have?" asked Devlin.

"We have caretakers who go every other week to clean and keep an eye on things. If anyone had attempted a break-in in the last two weeks we would have known," replied Phyllis. "Besides, the homes are held by a Trust. Someone would need to be very well connected to find out we owned all of them," she concluded.

Lola went to the desk to retrieve a piece of paper and a pen. She sat in the chair Devlin had vacated and prepared to write.

"We actually only need to write one note and send it the way we learned at school. It will find its way to whoever it's addressed to, no matter where they are," she explained. "What should we write in the note?" she asked.

They discussed the matter and Lola read the note back to them for validation:

"*Dear Dad,*

I really hope you're alive and well. After you left on July 6, 2020, I was summoned to the Academy, a school for Travelers. While I was there for a two-week Summer Program, I met an eighteen-year-old boy called Devlin who turned out to be my half-brother. Did you know? Did you send him a key and a marble in 2015?

Phyllis found a two-sided pocket watch in your room on August 7, 2020. Did you drop it accidentally? Do you need it back? People are looking for the watch and the marble, so we have sent them away for safekeeping. You'll know where.

Devlin would like to meet you. Phyllis and I miss you. If you can, please tell us where and when to meet you. If you fold your response exactly the way I did and address it to anyone of us, the letter will Travel to us instantly! How cool is that!

All our love,

Lola, Devlin, and Phyllis."

When everyone was satisfied, Lola folded the letter the way she was taught, addressed it to Simon Evers, and waited. The air swirled, the note launched up and disappeared.

"And now we wait," said Devlin.

26

DISNEY

At breakfast, Lola reminded Phyllis and Devlin that the Headmaster was waiting for their decision about the artifacts.

"I'll write to him immediately. I'm getting good at folding the letters!" said Phyllis proudly. "I'll also call Edward to ask him to check the Vault for the items we sent," she said, getting up. "While I'm doing that, I'd like you to think of somewhere you'd like to go for a few days," she said as she left the Sunroom.

With Jackson and Marie busy training John and Sally in the house, there would be no opportunity to discuss Traveling matters or study the Archives. They might as well use the time to do some family Traveling.

"I have never been to Disney World either," said Devlin. "And I enjoyed being at the beach," he added. "Perhaps we could combine both; they are in Florida, correct?" he asked Lola.

"Yes, they are. Do you like to go on rollercoasters?" she asked him.

"I love rollercoasters. I went to Liseberg in Gothenburg last year with my friends and it was an amazing experience!" he replied.

"Great, I don't know how Phyllis feels about amusement parks, but it's only a few days and there is apparently something for everyone," she said. Taking out her phone, Lola opened up the Maps app and looked up Disney World. She showed it to Devlin.

"Disney World is a city!" he exclaimed, zooming into the various parks within it.

"Yeah, but it's not close to the beach. Maybe we could go to the beach separately. We could go to a different beach every day for a year if we wanted!" said Lola, laughing.

Phyllis came back into the room and asked what was so funny and Lola explained.

"Disney World, an interesting choice for a couple of teenagers. But one I have to agree with. It's such a magical place, and no child should miss the opportunity to visit with Mickey Mouse!" she said. "Okay, Disney World it is. Why don't you two book us a suite for three nights, starting tonight, and park hopper passes until Thursday. We'll come home Thursday after dinner. That gives us the rest of the day to pack and prepare. Check-in will be at three p.m. and we can relax by the pool, get dinner and watch a parade later tonight."

"You've been there before?" asked Lola.

"Of course! But not in quite a while, I'm sure there's even more to see and do now!" she replied.

"How will we get there?" asked Devlin.

"We'll take a door directly to the hotel. There are usually lots of gardens and wooded areas around Disney hotels. Book it online with the family card, Devlin. And take the dining package as well, and whatever else you want. The works!" she exclaimed.

"But won't John and Sally wonder where we are?" asked Lola.

"We'll tell them, of course," replied Phyllis.

"But won't John and/or Jackson expect to drive us to the airport?" asked Devlin.

"Yes, I see your point," replied Phyllis, thinking.

They sat there for a minute trying to come up with a plan.

"We could ask Jackson to drive us to the airport and leave from one of the bathrooms," suggested Lola.

"No, not the airport. There are too many security cameras," said Phyllis. "But the train station here in Williamsburg would do nicely.

There's a small wooded area across the street. We'll just wait until Jackson's gone and cross the street," said Phyllis.

Lola and Devlin looked unsure. "I've been doing this a long time, trust me!" said Phyllis. "Now go online and book us a great adventure! I need to speak with John and Sally before we go and attend to a few personal matters," she added, setting down her napkin and rising from the table. "I'll see you at lunch," she said as she left.

"Let's go to the Schoolroom and use the big computer," suggested Lola.

"Good idea," replied Devlin.

They spent the rest of the morning assembling their three-night, four-day trip to Disney World. Phyllis had said the works, and that's what they got. Because Devlin wanted to be as close to nature as possible, they chose the Animal Kingdom Resort. Since they knew Phyllis liked her privacy, they settled on a two-bedroom villa in the Kidani village with a Savanna view which meant they could view thirty species of animals, like giraffes, zebras, antelopes, and ostriches, roaming right outside their window. With deluxe online check-in, they could Travel directly to the room and use their phones to unlock the room, enter the theme parks, and redeem their meal plan. They could arrive as early as two o'clock. Easy peasy.

They went to their rooms to pack and agreed to keep it to one bag. If they forgot something, they could simply come back for it. Lola brought her iPad to lunch so she could show Phyllis, but Phyllis preferred to be surprised. She too was all packed and ready.

John drove them to the train station as his first family practice run and Jackson stayed home to deal with the daily tasks. Since the family would be away for a few days, Jackson and Marie decided to have John and Sally work through the 'Summer' cleaning list, which was usually done later in August while Phyllis was traveling through Europe. Since she would be staying home with the children this year and both Jackson and Marie would have gone, this seemed like the perfect time to get most of it out of the way.

Meanwhile, the Evers had arrived in Orlando and were touring their villa in utter shock. As gorgeous as the pictures had been online, the reality was even better. Phyllis, who had been on safari in Africa, said it was almost like being there. They put their things away and went to explore the resort. They had a dip in the pool and a soak in the hot tub and still had plenty of time to relax before heading out to dinner. The food was incredible, of course, and Lola flipped out when they went to see the *Tree of Life Awakening*, a nighttime experience at Animal Kingdom.

The next three days were amazing. They went on all the thrill rides, watched all the shows they could manage, and took pictures with most of the main cartoon characters. Devlin and Lola were having the time of their lives and Phyllis admitted she was having more fun with them than she had with Simon, many, many years ago. Every night after dinner, they would soak their tired bodies in the hot tub and fall asleep in minutes.

Lola still found time for morning meditation and yoga. It was great having a villa. They had their own kitchen and she could make coffee right when she woke up. Meditating on a balcony overlooking the Savanna was out of this world. It was also easier to have breakfast at the villa, rather than going to the Main Lodge. No one wanted to cook, so they would put their order in the night before and room service delivered it promptly at seven. There was too much to do and they were all early risers.

On Wednesday morning, Lola and Devlin got their scripts from Tom. They agreed to open them at home. There was still no response from Simon.

When they came back after dinner on Thursday night, everyone agreed it was a memorable experience they would want to repeat, soon! They were able to Travel home directly since John and Sally had gone for the day and Jackson was off duty. They could always say they'd gotten a taxi if anyone asked.

27

ACTORS

On Friday morning Jackson went over a few more things with Devlin while Lola and Phyllis worked on Lola's part for Tom's party. The idea was that all the most influential people of the 20s would converge at a special party in an obscure Speakeasy in an undisclosed location. Artistic tempers would run high and drama would ensue.

Lola was to portray Zelda Sayre who, according to Wikipedia, was a novelist, short story writer, poet, dancer, painter, and socialite. Born in Montgomery, Alabama, she was married to F. Scott Fitzgerald, author of The Great Gatsby, portrayed by Tom.

"You'll get to practice your southern drawl!" exclaimed Phyllis. "What a great part to play. Zelda was a little more outgoing than you, and quite the trouble-maker, but you have much in common with her. It's a good choice for you. It'll get you out of your comfort zone!" said Phyllis with a wink.

She outfitted Lola with a rose-gold, sleeveless, knee-length sequined slip gown whose beaded fringe started at mid-thigh and was straight-cut with a drop waist. It was accented with a feather boa, rows upon rows of pearl necklaces of varying lengths, a headdress complete with jewels and feathers, and a pair of moiré dance shoes. Lola and

Phyllis were conveniently the same size, and Lola marveled at her appearance in the mirror.

"You look fabulous!" exclaimed Phyllis.

"Isn't this dress a little short? Shouldn't I be wearing stockings?" asked Lola, tugging on the fringe in the hopes it would lengthen.

"It the perfect length for a flapper!" replied Phyllis, amused.

"What's a flapper?" asked Lola, warily.

"A flapper was a young woman in the 20s who wore short skirts, bobbed her hair, listened to jazz, and refused to follow the rules regarding acceptable social behavior," replied Phyllis, wistfully. "Ah, to have lived in the roaring 20s!" she added dreamily.

"Well, all I need now is a gimlet and cigarette holder!" joked Lola.

Phyllis put her hands to her face and vanished into her closet, only to come out with a jeweled cigarette holder!

"It wouldn't be complete without it! And you wouldn't be drinking a gimlet. It would be either a Bees Knees, a Sidecar, or a Gin Rickey," she answered matter-of-factly.

"I don't even want to know what those are," said Lola, putting up her hands and shrieking when her dress hiked up and she felt a draft on her bottom. "I can't wear this, it's indecent!"

"Don't be ridiculous. Girls wear less than that in nightclubs today. You'll be fine. Besides, everyone else will be dressed like this. You'll fit right in! Let's look at the list of characters," said Phyllis with excitement.

"Tom plays my husband. Devlin is Albert Einstein," started Lola.

"Oh, lovely, that will be easy for him!" exclaimed Phyllis, motioning for Lola to continue.

"Clara is portraying Coco Chanel, a good choice for her. Lenora will be Louise Brooks, whoever that is," continued Lola, reading down the list.

"She was a sexy movie star," explained Phyllis.

"Yup, that would fit Lenora. Sara will play Mary Pickford who, I believe, was a very famous actress. Colin is to play Al Capone, and James is portraying Charlie Chaplin. There are other characters, but I don't know the people playing them," concluded Lola, giving the list to Phyllis, who nodded enthusiastically.

"This is amazing. I'll have to hire this playwright for a party here sometime," said Phyllis, clearly serious. "Anyhow, it says here if you were the murderer or the murder victim, it would be clearly written on your fact sheet. I guess you're off the hook!" said Phyllis.

Lola took one last look at herself and sighed. She had to admit she looked good. And this was a part she was playing, so she would have to be brave and go with it.

"Okay, I guess I can do this," she said with resignation.

"All we need now is to make your hair appear shorter. I have just the thing," she said and ran into her bathroom. Phyllis was obviously enjoying this more than Lola. She smiled at her aunt when she came back with a bag full of hair accouterments and let her fuss with her hair for as long as she wanted. While she did, Lola practiced her southern drawl. Later she would look up Zelda Fitzgerald to get a feel of the character.

After lunch, Phyllis spent some time with Devlin to prepare for his part. He was very happy about being Albert Einstein, a character he could identify with. The costume was easy: a black three-piece suit they borrowed from Simon since Devlin's clothes looked brand new. The cravat was tied differently, and they added a fedora to the outfit. The last piece was the mustache. Where Phyllis had gotten such a convincing mustache was a mystery, but once Devlin's hair was slicked back, with a touch of sprayed on gray at the temples, the effect was believable.

"I look like Albert Einstein when he accepted his first Nobel Prize," he exclaimed, astonished.

"And a very handsome one, too," replied Phyllis, smiling proudly while brushing invisible lint from his jacket. "Come look at my father's portrait in the hall, the resemblance is striking with the mustache," she said, pulling on his sleeve towards the hall.

They stood in front of her parents' wedding portrait. Devlin did look like her father, more so than Simon. He felt a warm rush in his stomach at seeing confirmation that he belonged here, in this house, to this family. Overcome with emotion, he took Phyllis' hand but said nothing. She squeezed his fingers in silent understanding.

"All right, you're all set, Albert," she quipped.

They went back to his room to pack his overnight bag, and then Phyllis said she was going to rest before dinner.

Friday night, they had a small going away party for Marie and Jackson. It was Marie's last day and Jackson was leaving for his European tour the next day. Although Phyllis protested that she should be doing the cooking, Marie insisted on making Phyllis' favorite meal: rosemary lamb chops with homemade mint jelly. Served with roasted garlic fingerling potatoes and fresh corn. She also made Jackson's favorite dessert: hot date-nut blondies served with vanilla ice cream. Marie would be missed, but she assured them that Sally was an accomplished cook and they would do fine.

It was a fun evening and both Marie and Jackson were looking forward to their upcoming trip. Marie was going on a river cruise in the Douro Valley, between Spain and Portugal. She and her husband were wine lovers and the cruise would take them to more than twenty wineries up and down the coast. Jackson had no set itinerary, but was starting his trip in London where he knew some friends from boarding school.

There were more than a few tears shed as they said their goodbyes. Marie promised to send postcards from her trip and a letter now and again to keep in touch. Jackson promised to check-in with a text message at least once a week so Phyllis wouldn't worry. He was like a son to her and she was going to miss him.

Jackson and Devlin shook hands. He and Phyllis went into the Library to give Jackson a moment alone with Lola.

"When does your flight leave?" she asked, stalling for time.

"At ten tonight," he replied.

"Do you have a ride?" Lola asked.

"Yeah, Bonnie is driving me on her way to her grandmother's," he said.

Lola shuffled her feet and looked at the floor. A few weeks ago, she thought she was going to marry this boy, and now he was leaving and they felt like strangers.

He took a step towards her and lifted her chin with his finger.

"I'll be back in two weeks," he said and wrapped her in a bear hug.

He knew she was thinking of the more permanent goodbyes they would be saying when he came back and they both left for school. Already things were different. Despite her feelings for Tom, there was a pull between her and Jackson. Lola had chalked it up to teenage hormones and the fact that they'd spent so much time together in such a short time. Either way, it felt wrong when he was gone.

"I'll miss you," she said simply.

"Me, too," he replied. He kissed her forehead and left the Mansion without looking back.

28

PARTY

Phyllis decided to accompany Lola and Devlin to Tom's house in Cork. Neither of them objected, in fact, they were relieved. Tom was outside with his mother at eleven greeting guests as they arrived. Lola and Devlin were among the first to arrive, so few people were on hand to witness their arrival with a parent.

Tom greeted Phyllis politely and introduced her to his mother, Arabella, who frowned upon hearing her name. Phyllis waved it away and said, "We're Americans, we never follow the rules!" Tom's mother smiled and drew Phyllis into the house for a quick tour while Tom greeted Lola and Devlin. The boys shook hands and clapped each other on the shoulder in a half hug. Then Tom approached Lola, took both her hands, and kissed each one in turn.

"It's good to see you," he said.

"It's good to see you, too," replied Lola, smiling shyly at him.

"You remember my sister Tabitha," he said. "You met at the picnic and she's Lenora's friend," he added.

They said 'Hi' and were soon joined by Phyllis and Arabella. Tom introduced Lola and Devlin.

"It's nice to see you again," said Lola, nervously. She wondered how much Tom had said about her.

"How lovely to see you again, Lola," said Arabella. Tabitha piped up and said with a wink, "Tom has been going on and on about you all week." Tom's eyes bulged out of his head and his gaze shot daggers at his sister.

Lola and Devlin said goodbye to Phyllis, and then Tabitha took them to their rooms so they could drop off their things and unpack. She told them to join everyone outside when they were ready, where a buffet-lunch would be laid out under the canopy.

"We'll have a group tour after lunch," she said before she left.

When Lola got to her room, she found Sara was already there. The girls greeted each other with warm hugs and happy shrieks. The room had two other bunks and Sara said Lenora and Clara would be rooming with them as well.

"Looks like we're roommates for life!" said Sara.

"What a great surprise!" replied Lola. "I wonder who Devlin is rooming with. Let's go see."

They walked down the hall and knocked on the door where she had left Devlin a few minutes before. Devlin opened the door to utter mayhem. Colin and James were there, talking a mile-a-minute about some sort of wizard exploits.

"Hey, guys," exclaimed Lola.

"Lola! And Sara!" said James, grabbing both girls for a group hug. Colin kissed their cheeks and said, "Looking as lovely as ever, ladies."

"Who's the poor chap who'll be sharing a room with you lot?" asked Sara with a chuckle.

"It's Tom, actually. He's given his room to his uncle and thought it would be more fun to room with us," answered James.

"Fantastic!" exclaimed Devlin.

"Okay, we're in the room on the other side of the bathroom. We'll see you later, then," said Sara, pulling Lola out of the room and into the hall.

"Those boys are loud!" she said.

They went back to their room and hung their party outfits in the closet. A few minutes later, the door opened and both Lenora and Clara came in. There was more shrieking and hugging, and some jumping up and down. They too unpacked and hung up their party dresses. Everyone marveled at the dresses. Phyllis had been right—Lola's was the most modest of the outfits! They had a bit of a chat to catch up on the last two weeks. Lola shared information about their trip to Disney World, but nothing else.

At noon, they headed back outside, with the boys in tow.

They were introduced to the other guests. There were Tom's friends from the Academy, a few cousins, and a few of Tabitha's Academy friends. People assembled plates of food at the buffet and chatted. By one-thirty, all the guests had arrived. Tom clinked his glass to get everyone's attention.

"I'd like to introduce the mastermind behind this evening's events. This is my uncle, Aidan McCarthy, three-time Irish Film & Television Academy Award winner and two-time American Academy Award nominee," he said.

Everyone applauded the screenwriter, and he raised his hands in thanks.

"Hello, everyone! It's a pleasure to be here, and I had a grand time writing tonight's 'play.' Though everyone has a part, you don't have a set role, unless you are the murderer or the victim. The victim has no idea when, how, or even why they will be murdered. The murderer does not yet know who the victim is, or how they will be murdered. He or she will be told as the evening unfolds to maintain the suspense.

"I have given myself the role of Eugene O'Neill—he was a famed playwright in the 1920s. I'll tell you all about him later tonight. My sister, Arabella, will portray the illustrious Josephine Baker.

"Here's how the evening is going to unfold. The afternoon is yours to do as you like. Tom and Tabitha will provide a list of activities. At six sharp, you should report to the foyer where you will be provided with name badges. We'll have drinks, and I will introduce myself as Eugene O'Neill. I will introduce each character and provide a short bio. We will then proceed to the dining room; please sit in your assigned seat and converse with your dinner companions in character as much as possible. After dinner, you will return here, to the canopy tent which will have been transformed into our 1920s Speakeasy. Once inside, you will not be permitted to leave until the evening is concluded; that is, until the murderer has been found! Unless there is an emergency, of course. Should such a situation arise, please see me or my sister.

"The canopy will be enchanted, no Traveling allowed! Restrooms will be available inside. Any questions?"

Michael, one of Tom's friends, raised his hand. "Will there be other people in the Speakeasy with us?" he asked.

"Good question. Yes, there will be staff and entertainers, but they will not be part of the plot," replied Aidan.

Clara raised her hand. "How long will the plot last?" she asked.

"That depends on your detective skills! I promise it won't be too difficult, but there will be a bit of a challenge," was his response. "I don't, however, foresee it lasting very much beyond eleven. The plot should be done by then, and the staff and entertainers will leave. Should some of you wish to keep the party going, it is entirely at your discretion," he concluded.

There were no more questions. He bowed and left. Everyone applauded and Tom came back to the center.

"Tomorrow, we'll have a brunch buffet set up here in the canopy from eleven to one. Feel free to sleep in! For those early birds, you'll find coffee, tea, and assorted snacks as early as seven. Should you feel like a walk, we have a lovely trail that leads to the Channel just behind that hedge," he said, pointing to a tall hedge behind him. "Otherwise, you can sit by the pool or in the garden. We have many chairs and benches to accommodate you all," he continued. "In the afternoon, we'll go down to the Channel to swim, go out in the canoes, kayaks, or paddle boats, and just chill out. Sound good?" he asked and everyone cheered.

"Feel free to join me at the pool," he said, pointing in the opposite direction. "I'll be there as soon as I've had a private chat with my girl," he said, walking towards Lola. There were whistles and catcalls and Lola turned a new shade of red she had yet to wear.

Seeing her friend's discomfort, Sara shooed everyone away and soon they scattered back to their rooms to change for the pool party. Lola mouthed *Thank you* and Sara left arm in arm with Devlin.

Once they were alone, Lola punched Tom in the arm. He yelped and asked why she was hitting him.

"You put me on the spot. I was mortified!" she said in dismay.

"I'm sorry, Lola. I just wanted everyone to see how lucky I am to have such a beautiful girlfriend," he said.

Lola eyed him and put a hand on her hip. "I don't recall having that conversation," she said.

"What conversation would that be?" he asked, innocently.

"The one where we decided we were a couple," she said, still eyeing him suspiciously.

"Well now, that was a given," he stated, as though it should have been obvious.

"I'm sorry. I'm new at this. What clue did I miss?" she asked.

Tom looked genuinely surprised. "We kissed. On the lips, with tongue!" he cried. "Are you telling me you go around French kissing with every boy you meet?" he asked, clearly affronted now. Lola smiled. *He was new to this too*, she thought. She threw her arms around him and hugged him. "I missed you, Tom O'Callahan," she said with a sigh.

"Now that's better," he replied, wrapping his arms around her and kissing the top of her head. "But I'll be wanting an answer to that question," he reminded her.

"What question?" she asked, nuzzling into his neck.

"Do you go around French kissing every boy you meet?" he repeated.

She stepped back and looked him straight in the eye. "You are the second boy I've French-kissed and, honestly, I hope you're the last!" she said earnestly.

A huge grin appeared on his face and he bent down to kiss her lightly on the lips. "You're my first, Lola Evers and, honestly, I hope you're the last!" he said and kissed her again. He lingered this time. He took her hand and walked her over to one of the benches along the path to the Channel. It was under a weeping willow, so it gave them a little privacy.

Once they were seated, Tom caressed her face as he looked upon it in wonder. He inched closer and kissed her cheek, her temple, her forehead, then back down again the other side of her face. Lola grew warm and took hold of his shirt to draw him closer. Her lips touched his, tentatively at first, then she applied more pressure and their lips parted. The kiss deepened and they awkwardly tried to get closer while sitting side by side on the bench. As the kiss grew steamier, they heard someone clear their throat nearby and pulled away.

It was Tom's uncle Aidan.

"Sorry to interrupt, kids, but I believe your guests are waiting for you by the pool, Tom," he said with a barely concealed smile.

"Yes, uncle Aidan. Thank you for reminding me," he said, getting up and taking Lola's hand to assist her. His uncle chuckled and made his way towards the Channel with a towel on one shoulder, a book under his arm, and a beer in hand.

"We should get changed and meet at the pool," said Tom. "I'll walk you to your room."

They went inside and Tom left Lola in front of her room and went to his own room to change. When she came out, he was waiting for her and they went to the pool together. He told her about his trip with his family and how Aidan was moving in with them to help out now that his father was gone.

When they got to the pool, the music stopped and everyone yelled, "Surprise!" and then started singing Happy Birthday. There was a huge cake on a trolley with sixteen candles and a bunch of sparklers. Tom made a wish and blew them out. Everyone applauded and the music resumed. Tom's mother started cutting the cake and offered pieces to those who wanted them. They had fun by the pool and played SUP Warriors, a game where each opponent stood on a paddleboard and, with padded oars, tried to knock the other off his or her board. The reigning champion was Tabitha, who had likely had a lot of practice.

By four o'clock, most of the girls had fled for their rooms to shower, change, and prepare for their roles. There was no point in the boys leaving before five since all the bathrooms would be occupied with hysterical females applying layers of makeup through a haze of perfume and hairspray.

29

SPEAKEASY

A t six o'clock, everyone was in costume and in character. They assembled in the foyer where a photographer was on hand to take their pictures with various frames set up around the room. Everyone was buzzing with excitement. Waiters circulated with trays and served a champagne punch and hors d'oeuvres. Arabella and Aidan went to each guest and affixed their name tag, complimenting them on their hair, their costume, or added accessories they had chosen to portray their character.

Dinner in the dining room was a lavish affair. Everyone was seated at one extensive table, nine guests on either side with Arabella and Aidan at either end. Once introductions were made, the first of the six-course meal was served and the play began.

Lola was seated between Salvador Dali, whose mustache was spot on, and Charles Lindbergh, sporting a genuine-looking aviator cap and goggles on his head. Both were handsome young men who had clearly researched their characters and were able to carry on riveting conversations. Lola thought she made a convincing Zelda Fitzgerald. When posed a question she didn't know how to respond to, she simply took a drag on her cigarette holder and exhaled imaginary smoke and saying things like, "Oh darling, how very uninteresting," and turning her head to her other companion with a flick of her wrist. This got peals of laughter from Clara and Lenora, seated on either side of her companions.

Devlin was having a marvelous time as Albert Einstein, trying to explain the law of photoelectric effect, for which he won his first Nobel prize, to Coco Chanel, the first to design pants for women, and Alice Paul, a famous women's activist.

Meanwhile, Tom was engrossed in a conversation with Ernest Hemingway and Walt Disney, though Lola could not hear the details.

After the final course of dessert and nuts was completed, almost two hours later, everyone was served a glass of wine. Sweet wine for the ladies and port for the gentlemen. Arabella rose and beckoned the ladies to follow her into the drawing-room while the gentlemen stayed in the dining room to smoke cigars and discuss manly topics. This short interlude lasted no longer than thirty minutes, during which the guests were allowed to use the restrooms, or return to their rooms for any wardrobe changes.

At nine o'clock, the guests were sent to the white canopy tent outside. The side panels had been drawn to enclose the space entirely. From the outside, there was no sound. Two doormen, dressed like gangsters and holding what looked like real machine guns, greeted the guests. There was an actual door. One of the gangsters had a list, and the other held a key which presumably opened the door. Each guest had to provide their name and was sent individually. Lola peered nervously at her friends, unsure.

"Go on, Zelda! You're a flapper, you've got this!" said Al Capone aka Colin.

Lola walked through the door and was instantly transported to an underground Speakeasy. It was unclear if passing through the door had let to another location or if the canopy had been enchanted. Either way, this was a whole new world.

The room was about fifteen feet wide by thirty feet long, and it appeared to be located in a somewhat damp basement cellar. With low ceilings, exposed brick walls covered with black and white photographs of tonight's guests, and a two-man bar at the back, the most impressive feature was the five-player jazz ensemble at the front of the room and the four crescent-shaped booths positioned in such a way that everyone could see the band yet still observe the other patrons. The center space provided enough room for dancing.

There were no windows and no visible emergency exits. On either side of the bar were two doors marked *Gents* and *Dolls*. Lola was about to turn back, but the door she had come in from was no longer there. All twenty guests were in the Speakeasy and were taking seats in the booths. F. Scott Fitzgerald was waving her over with a smile. Lola took a deep breath and reminded herself that this was a party. It was supposed to be fun.

When the band's number ended, everyone clapped and Josephine Baker took the stage. She called out to one of the guests, Duke Ellington, to join her and they danced as the band played. Soon, other couples joined them and Tom was urging Lola towards the dance floor. She resisted at first, then remembered how confidently he led her before and let him drag her onto the dance floor. This was by far much easier to do, and soon Lola was enjoying herself. Josephine and Duke demonstrated how to do the Foxtrot, the Charleston, and the Brazilian Samba, and the guests gamely followed along.

Waitresses dressed like showgirls carried trays with straps around their necks and brought refreshments to the tables. Sidecars and Gin Rickeys were indeed being served, though Lola didn't hear talk of Bee's Knees being available. When she asked for a glass of club soda, it was served with ice and whiskey and was called a Highball. She decided to stick with the Sidecar, which was delicious if potent.

At some point, she danced with Aidan and asked if it was possible to get a drink without alcohol.

"Sure, just ask for a Prohibition Daisy," he said in her ear.

"What's in it?" she asked suspiciously.

"It's basically a fruit smoothie. Pineapple, orange, raspberry, and lime juice," he explained and then returned her to her table when the song was over.

Lola ordered it and the waitress didn't bat an eye. When the drink arrived, she sniffed it but couldn't tell if there was alcohol in it. Nor could she tell after tasting it, but it was divine and she was thirsty. She was happily sipping her mocktail and tapping her foot to the music when the lights went out; the musicians faltered but kept playing. Someone lit a lantern at another table. There was a blood-curdling scream and the music stopped. Lola grabbed for whoever was next to her; hopefully, it was Tom or Devlin. Then she remembered either one of them could be the murderer, but she was not the victim and this was only a game. She relaxed a little.

The lights returned and everyone started talking at the same time and looking everywhere for the victim and asking who had screamed.

The victim was spread-eagled in the middle of the dance floor. It was Louise Brooks, her auburn hair fanned out around her face.

"Nobody touch her!" yelled Eugene O'Neill, aka Tom's uncle, who asked everyone to back up a little and let him pass.

As he approached the victim, he eyed Ernest Hemingway suspiciously. He had been dancing with Louise only moments ago.

"It wasn't me; I swear!" he cried, hand in the air and shaking his head in distress. He was convincing in his role.

Eugene took a piece of chalk from his pocket and traced the outline of her body, then drew a perimeter circle around the body. After that, he invited everyone to observe Louise closely to spot any clues or evidence. They had five minutes.

The two barmen produced a chaise and placed it in front of the band. Louise, aka Lenora, was picked up and deposited on the chaise where she would remain until her killer was found. She had been told that she did not need to remain corpse like for the rest of the evening. Rather, once she had been examined visually by the guests, she could open her eyes and recline at her leisure.

The band started playing slow jazz pieces in the background. Guests returned to their seats and were provided with pen and paper and were permitted to discuss the murder with those at their table. They pooled their list of clues and evidence. Then they sought motive and opportunity. Finally, they drew up a list of three potential suspects. Each table, or team, could present one suspect at a time. After all four tables had presented their first suspects, Arabella told them whether someone had got it right. After the first round, they were still looking. Lists of suspects were amended after the first round and extra clues were added.

After the second round of suspects, they still hadn't found the killer. People were stumped. Eugene suggested that two people from each table move to another table to make new teams. When the final round of suspects was presented, they had a winner. The killer had been Charles Lindbergh, and the motive had been as simple as could be, Louise had rejected him and laughed at his advances.

Everyone applauded. Arabella introduced the members of the band, who bowed and played one final song. The waitresses came out for a bow as well and left through a door that hadn't been there until minutes ago. The barmen were introduced and applauded, but only one of them left, followed by the band members. When he produced a calling card from his vest pocket, a copy also appeared in everyone's hand. It said: Ivan Lazarus - Illusionist.

With a snap of his fingers he was gone and so was the Speakeasy. They were all standing inside the white canopy tent, sitting at the same tables and chairs they had used at lunch.

The guests wore identical astonished expressions. It took a minute for everyone to react, and then they were all talking at once. Some were clapping, some whooping, and others were still too stunned to say much of anything. Lola was among those who just sat there staring out around her in utter shock.

"That was EPIC!" shouted Colin as he high-fived Tom. "You've outdone yourself!"

The guys crowded around Tom, congratulating him on the amazing party, and slapping him on the back.

Arabella called for everyone's attention. She and Aidan were going to say a few words before retiring for the evening, but the kids were applauding and hollering their appreciation and it took a while to calm them down.

"You are most welcome," replied Arabella. "My thanks must go to my brother, since without his genius and contacts, we wouldn't have been able to pull this off," she said smiling up at him. The teens applauded once more.

"You have been a wonderful cast and I had a great time. You have Ivan's card should you wish to plan a party with him. I enjoyed myself so much that I would consider doing this again in the future. With a different theme, of course!"

They said goodnight and left Tom and his guests to continue the party without them. It was eleven o'clock on the nose. Impeccable timing.

30

STILLNESS

"The problem with being a morning person is that by eleven o'clock at night, you are exhausted," said Lola to Tom after he caught her trying to sneak out of the tent. "And I had a glass of champagne punch before dinner, a glass of sweet wine at dinner, and a sidecar in the Speakeasy. I'm tired and I feel woozy," she said holding on to Tom's forearm.

He nodded and helped her outside the tent where the fresh Cork air had wonderful restorative powers. She breathed it in and her shoulders relaxed. She realized she'd been on edge all evening, worried about not being able to get out if there had been an emergency.

"I think I might be a little claustrophobic," she admitted. "As amazing as the evening was, I'm glad to be out of that cellar and the tent. Will you walk with me a little before I head to bed?" she asked.

He gave her his arm and they strolled down the path to the Channel. When they got there, Lola was surprised to see they had to cross a road to get to the Channel. She was expecting a deck or beach overlooking the lake. It was dark and they couldn't see much, so they walked back, hand in hand.

As they neared the house, Tom asked if she was feeling better or she needed anything.

"Yes, I feel better. It's nothing that a good night's sleep won't cure. I'll have a large glass of water and head straight to bed. It's a good thing you thought to add earplugs to your list of things to bring; I'm pretty sure the girls will make enough ruckus to wake the dead when they get back from the party," she said with a laugh.

He opened his arms and she walked into them gratefully. They held each other for a long time until they heard someone clear her throat behind them.

"I'm sorry to interrupt," said Sara, awkwardly. "But you're standing in front of our door," she explained.

Lola and Tom stepped apart and kissed lightly on the lips. "Good night," said Lola.

"Sweet dreams," replied Tom as he moved out of the way to let Sara pass. That's when they noticed Devlin leaning against the wall behind them. He and Sara had already said their goodnights outside and Devlin had walked her to her door. He smiled and grabbed Tom by the arm and led him back to the party.

Lola and Sara got ready for bed. They had chosen to sleep in the same bunk, thinking they were less likely to be disturbed by Clara and Lenora when they got back. Who knew what time they'd return. Sara had called dibs on the top bunk. That was fine with Lola. She preferred the bottom bunk. She grabbed an extra blanket and stuffed the edges under the top mattress, and it draped around her bed like curtains. She hated the idea of people looking at her sleep. At The Academy, they had the bookcase between them to act as a wall, and not once had Sara gotten up before her or gone to bed after her. She felt safer in her little cocoon. She said goodnight to Sara and popped in her earplugs and settled into the strange bed. She was tired and perhaps a little drunk, so she fell asleep quickly.

She awoke in the night, unable to tell what had awoken her. It was still dark out, not yet morning. She checked her phone; it was three-thirty. She lifted her blanket curtain and checked the other bunk bed and saw both Clara and Lenora fast asleep. Poking her head out, she looked up and confirmed Sara was still in bed. She grabbed her water bottle and took one long pull and settle back onto her pillow, but sleep eluded her. She took the earplugs out and placed them under the pillow and decided to go to the bathroom since she was awake. She sat up and launched her feet out of her cocoon and into her slippers. Her head and body followed and as she rose, something fell to the floor. It wasn't her phone since she was holding it. Touching the screen and casting the light onto the floor, Lola froze. It was a Traveling letter with her name on it. She snatched it up, tiptoed out into the hall and headed for the bathroom. Once inside, she turned on the light and locked the door. The letter had been folded as usual, but a wax seal was holding the folds together. It was stamped with the Evers seal. She cracked the seal and unfolded the letter.

In the center of the paper were three words written in a hand that Lola had seen before.

Come home. Immediately.

Lola checked both sides of the paper. That's all it said. But it was clear. Simon had responded and he wanted her to come home, now. She had to get Devlin. But she didn't want to wake the whole room, let alone the whole house. She took a deep breath and closed her eyes. She slowed her breathing and cleared her mind. It wasn't easy.

Devlin! she thought. *Devlin, wake up!* she tried again. She waited a for long minute. Then, she tried to scream in her mind and hoped she hadn't actually screamed out loud. *Devlin, wake up. It's an emergency!*

She heard him mumble. "What?" from the other side of the bathroom wall and quickly added, *Shhh. It's Lola, in your mind. I'm in the bathroom next door, come meet me.*

She heard him bump his head and curse. *I guess he slept in the bottom bunk too,* she thought to herself. She heard shuffling and then a light knock on the bathroom door. She unlocked it, opened the door, checked the hall, and closed it behind him. He was holding a Traveling letter too. Seeing she had one too, and hers was open, he cracked the seal and opened his letter. It was identical to hers.

"It's Dad. He's home," said Lola. "We should go. Now," she whispered quickly.

"Are we sure?" he asked. "Have you seen this seal before?" he inquired.

"It's our family logo," she answered.

"But I have never seen Phyllis use it," replied Devlin. "It is the middle of the night. Surely this could have waited until morning," he said suspiciously.

"Perhaps he thought we'd only see the letters in the morning," said Lola.

"We have two options," replied Devlin. "We can send one of these letters to Phyllis and see what she replies," he started. "Or send her a text message," he added. "Either way, if it is an emergency, she'll be up and respond immediately," he concluded.

"And if she doesn't then it's not an emergency. We'll go back to bed and call her in the morning," said Lola.

"Agreed," said Devlin.

"I prefer the letter idea, but I don't have a pen," said Lola with a pained expression.

"Oh, neither do I," replied Devlin. "I guess we'll have to send a text message then," he said.

Lola took out her phone and took a picture of the letter and the broken seal and sent them to Phyllis' phone with the following text message:

Phyllis! Devlin and I just got this. Is it legit? Did you or Dad send it?

They waited. And waited. Then her phone buzzed with a response.

Your father sent it. Come home.

The bathroom seemed a little snug to open a Traveling door inside. They opened the door, closed the light, and crept down the hall to some sort of parlor. It was empty. Lola whipped out her key, opened the door, and walked into the upper hall, Devlin close behind. They walked to Phyllis's room and knocked. There was no answer. They tried the handle and it turned. The room was dark.

"Phyllis?" asked Lola, her hand going for the light switch. When the lights turned on, she heard Devlin gasp. Lola turned to look where

Devlin was looking. There was someone in the room. It was neither Phyllis nor Simon. The man was seated at Phyllis's vanity, absently pawing through her things.

"What have you done with Phyllis?" yelled Lola, angrily taking a step closer to the man.

Devlin grabbed her arm to restrain her. He had noticed something Lola had not. The man had a gun.

"Your aunt isn't home. No one's home. I had time to search the Mansion top to bottom, but I'm afraid I haven't found what I was looking for. But I did find this ring in your father's desk," he said showing them the gold ring with the family crest. "It was easy to imitate your father's handwriting from his notebooks, and your aunt really should lock her phone screen," he said, pulling out Phyllis' phone from his pocket.

"Who are you? What do you want?" asked Devlin, keeping a protective arm around his sister and wondering how he could get them out of this. The man was holding a gun. There was no way they could reach in under their shirts to get their keys fast enough.

"I think you know what I want. The watch and the marble, if you please," he said waving the gun at them.

The End

If you enjoyed this book, please consider leaving a review on

Amazon, Goodreads, or Bookbub.

Reviews help me reach new readers.

Read *The World Jumper*, the final book in *The Evers Series*!

Join my Newsletter for writing updates, sales and giveaways!

ABOUT THE AUTHOR

Positive, uplifting books and stories.

Marie-Hélène Lebeault is the author of *The Evers Series, Clarity Castle, What Happens Next? Readers Decide Which Story Becomes a Book, the Blood Magick Trilogy, Holiday Shifters, Ghost Stories, Defenders of the Realm, Utopia, Chronicles of the Starborne Cadets*, as well as a series of picture books called Fairy Grandmother. She lives in Canada with her grown children.

www.mhlebeault.com

Follow on Social Media, she'd love to hear from you!

facebook.com/mhlebeaultauthor
x.com/mhlebeault
instagram.com/mhlebeault
amazon.com/author/mhlebeault
bookbub.com/authors/marie-helene-lebeault
goodreads.com/mhlebeault
linkedin.com/in/mhlebeault
tiktok.com/@mhlebeaultauthor

ALSO BY THE AUTHOR

Legends Reborn (Fairytale Retellings)

A Curse of Snow and Ash

A Curse of Thorns and Slumber

A Curse of Glass and Shadows

A Curse of Iron and Roses

A Curse of Briars and Hearts

The Chronicles of the Starborne Cadets

Stars Beyond Realms

Shadows of Orion

Echoes of the Void

The Nebula's Heart

The Starborne Paradox

Defenders of the Realm

A Journey to Power

The Quest for the Emerald Rattleback

A Summer of Discovery

The Quest for the Sacred Tree

A Summer of Opposites

The Quest for the Phantom Feather

A Summer of Courage

The Quest for the Kraken's Ink

A Summer of Destiny

The Quest for the Cursed Mirrors

A Summer of Unity

Defenders of the Realm - Special Edition Hardcover Set

The Evers Series

The Ancestors' Key

The Academy

The Time Walker

The World Jumper

5th Anniversary Edition Omnibus

The Traveler's Handbook

The Lost Key

Blood Magick Trilogy

The Blood Mage

Blood Magick

Blood Legacy

Extended Edition Omnibus

Standalones

Clarity Castle

What Happens Next?

Ghost Stories

Holiday Shifters

Echoes of Tomorrow

Utopia

Picture Books

Fairy Grandmother: Millie Goes to Antarctica

Fairy Grandmother: Millie Goes to the North Pole

Fairy Grandmother: Millie Goes to China

Fairy Grandmother: Millie Goes to Africa

(Also available in French, Spanish, German, and Italian)

www.ingramcontent.com/pod-product-compliance
Lightning Source LLC
Chambersburg PA
CBHW030251270626
47156CB00021B/1536